Jour

By J D Wallace

For Lynn. Her journey was too short.

Published 2016 by JD Wallace

Through Libertate publishing

Books by J D Wallace

The Boarder

The Dragon That Guards The Center

A Lion At The Gate Of The Temple

Cat From The Second World

Journey Of The Four Ancients

Lucky Star Double Novella (winter 2016)

Jade and A Lucky Star

Rhyming Words with Carolyn Chau

The Scroll from the Second World

I was feeling uncharacteristically happy. This bliss was probably due to the gentle rain which spattered against the pane of my bedroom window. A faint impression of a smile was apparent in my reflection in the glass. I was looking out over the hillside musing on the places that life had taken me. The imaginings promised to be exhilarating.

Arianna and I had been making extensive studies of the scroll we had acquired in the second world. It had been written by a sorcerer we'd defeated some months ago. Progress was slow and steady but recently we became aware that the information contained in the document was not enough to solve our most pressing problem. Where was the final gate?

We had previously discovered four of the five primary gates through which an evil entity from another world had been slowly spreading corruption into our world. The scroll had promised to help us in our quest for the last gate.

I know you are asking yourself, "What is this evil and corruption?" Unfortunately, that is not as difficult a question to answer as I'd like to think. Please indulge me. These questions, and others will be answered in the pages of this book.

The sun had yet to peek above the horizon that morning. There was the beginning of light slowly spreading a soft glow over the valley to the east. The morning mist was clearing away and revealing the dark green of the lowland forest. Here on the side of the mountain was the place I'd called home for the last two years.

I stood looking out the window. Rain had been gently falling for the last hour or so. A quarter mile to the southeast, I could barely make out the bridge that I had crossed two years earlier. It seemed so long ago.

The sun was beginning to light the sky as dawn had begun. I could not see the sun as it rose above the distant horizon. It was obscured by the deep east coast clouds that served a steady and wonderful rain.

I've said before how much I love the rain. Over the last few years I had had reason to change my view but still clung desperately to the hope that somehow the world could be washed clean. Maybe the rain wasn't enough. My hope was, I could offer some small aid to the battle against the corruption which silently infused evil into the fabric of the world.

My room was large and comfortable. On three walls interrupted only by the door were bookshelves. These supported thousands of books, which once belonged to Zach Drakson. They covered a large array of topics from history to the arcane and occult. He would have been considered the world's authority on corruption had he still lived. I often thought of the day when he died. I wished I could have gotten to know him better.

Still we were similar in many ways. Both of us had intelligence and focus. We were determined and capable. The real difference between us was his general good nature. My nature was somewhat standoffish.

I suppose my personality was something of an advantage in the work that I had taken up. Being distant and unused to emotion seemed to insulate me somewhat from feelings. The truth was I still had a hard time understanding my emotions. Even after having gone through terror and adventures with several very close friends, I still felt alone most of the time.

This was something I'd dealt with most of my life. My parents were the type that seldom showed affection. They did feel love for me. Their own emotional retardation seemed to have been passed on to me. Either by nurture or nature I was very much like them.

To say I didn't feel emotion would be a stretch. I simply had no idea how to act when faced with it. It seemed easier to simply ignore the unfamiliar feeling and think my way through whatever situation presented itself. This had led to problems in the few relationships I'd had.

My only close girlfriend had resurfaced recently and helped get us through an adventure in a place we had come to call "The Second World" from the Navaho legend. Recently she had been translating the scroll that had become the focus of my work.

It seems simple when I think about it. I have always been meant to do this. My work, chosen not by me but by fate, if fate was a real thing. I suppose I should be angry. I remind myself all the time that I do not believe in fate.

I do believe in what I am called to do. I have accepted that I must do this job. I know that I am capable. I am in fact, one of a very few people that can perform the essentials of the job. In so many words, I have been raised to do this work.

Someday the rest of humanity will know what we have done. Perhaps they might think of us as guardians and protectors. It is more likely that they will think of us as insane. Even if anyone believed what happened, to do what we have done, is not a sign of good mental health.

Many have lived and died in the battle against evil. Our struggle has been, until now, against one very powerful evil that threatens to corrupt all life. Each time we venture out I think that we might be the last. In spite of my pessimistic nature, I offer myself one consolation. In fact, we have won many battles. We have also lost many friends.

The scroll could lead us to the final gateway. This gate, we must either gain control of, or close, in order to stem the flow of corruption into our world.

We had, as I said before, found four of the five primary passages in space time. Each linked the in-between realm of the rift and its consciousness to other worlds filled with wonders and dangers. There are many other gates, but the five primary gates could be used to insulate our world from the evil corruption of the being known only as the Master.

The Master wanted to use the rift to gain control of all worlds. If it could gain control of the passages through space, the Master could send its agents to any world and spread its influence.

The rift which I'd come to call Grieta, a Spanish word for crack or chasm, had begun to aid us in our quest to save the world from evil. It had helped intelligent creatures for centuries. Only now did we begin to understand the mentality behind Grieta.

By way of catching up anyone reading this without having read the earlier journals, first I will recap the events of the last two years. Though you may not believe, I ask you to keep an open mind. There is terror and wonder in the universe that most people will never know. My task is to see to it that you may never know of the horror we have faced.

When I first discovered the rift, I had been on a walking tour of New England. My purpose was to write a book on old churches in the area and to clear my head after the untimely death of my parents.

A little over two years ago, my parents were killed in a house fire. They'd left me with enough money for an easy life so I'd quit my position at a prestigious architectural office. That was when I'd started walking.

My purpose was to get away and clear my mind. I wanted to figure out what to do with my life. Up till then it had been less than rewarding. I figured I could write a book on old churches and accomplish the head clearing as a sort of vocational sabbatical.

I came into a small town in the foothills and stumbled upon a family that needed my help. Their father had been experimenting with a metaphysical doorway to other worlds when he'd somehow been corrupted by the evil that had, for centuries, been trying to spread into our world.

This was the Drakson family. The six siblings of the family had introduced me to the war against corruption and asked my help in stopping the creature that had been their father. He had died in an attempt to use the local rift portal to locate another gate, which he thought was open and allowing corruption access to our world.

Only Maria, the youngest sister, and I had survived. Her five siblings were killed one by one till I had stopped the creature that had been stalking them. I should say that it was more by luck than by any skill I had that I'd destroyed it.

We had become aware of a second gate that seemed to be actively used as a portal into our world by evil creatures. I'd been using a charm that offered a sort of divination by way of changes in its temperature as a response to questions, and a lens that allowed a person to see through the rift to locate other open rifts. This power seemed somewhat limited and though it worked, its ability to locate any particular gate, was not what I would call satisfactory.

The crux of the problem is that there is in fact an evil mentality, which resides in another world. It seeks control over all. It uses agents of evil to manipulate and corrupt life. By transferring a mentality into a living or dead host in our world it, can slowly spread its influence into our plane of existence.

Their father had been consumed by the corruption and transformed into a hideous undead monster which had murdered all but the youngest of the Drakson's before I had finally managed to defeat it. This was more by luck than design but it started me on the path.

I agreed to help Maria, the last surviving Drakson and began looking for the other open gateway by using the charm and lens that once belonged to her brother Zach. The charm was a sort of divining device, which answered questions by way of temperate changes in the metal of the offset gem in a gold hoop. The lens was created by Zach to create a sort of lock, which would prevent corruption from using any given gateway. It had other abilities as well, including the power to see across the rift into another portal, and it could transfer someone from portal to portal without the need of travelling in the rift itself.

I'd travelled through the south and then west, and had faced off against a corrupted creature in Atlanta.

My next stop was New Mexico. Upon arriving in Albuquerque, I was promptly ushered off the La Guera reservation by the local medicine chief and met a group of people that had been investigating some bizarre murders.

The murders turned out to have been committed by a cult dedicated to bringing the Master and its corruption into our world by way of a spider-like brain parasite. With the help of several new allies we'd managed to stop the plans of a group called the "Familia Arnea." They had been spreading a form of corruption which acted as a sort of brain spider parasite.

I encountered several other corrupted creatures before discovering the rift geode which had been split into two parts. Each part was now its own gateway connected to the other half.

During that investigation, I'd also discovered information about the five primary gates. At first I thought these might simply be five of the potentially thousands that might exist in our world. Later I began to suspect that these five gates were the primary contact points with the rift. Though others existed, these were the only ones that would allow transmission of a mentality into a host body in our world.

The other gates could be used for communication and even transfer of a physical form. Very few of the creatures from the realm of the master could exist in our world in physical form. Thus, the need to control these five gates.

Maria had lost her fiancé on an archeological dig in Southeast Asia a year before. After discovering the facts surrounding the strange happenings at the site we decided it was worth our time to interrupt our investigations and try to determine the fate of those members of the expedition that had been lost.

So after our adventures in New Mexico, we headed to Southeast Asia and uncovered the remains of a temple dedicated to destroying corruption. This temple had become corrupted and possessed with a spiritual stone monster which was difficult to destroy. Maria disconnected it from its source of power and in the process, we had rescued her lost fiancé who had disappeared there the year before.

What we discovered was no less than the third of the gates and a temple that had been completely overcome with corruption. What we thought were series of mishaps turned out to be sabotage by one of our party, resulting in many deaths. Finally, we managed to overcome the corrupting creature and restore the temple to use by our team.

Maria was reunited with Keith, her fiancé, when his mentality, which had been preserved by Grieta was joined with that of Conner, one of the members of our team. Keith's mind had been protected by Grieta and saved as a sort of ghost. One of our companions, Conner, was close to death after an encounter with corruption. Grieta melded Conner's mentality with that of Keith and saved them both. Two of our companions had also given their lives and transferred their mentalities into the temple to become guardians of the rift in the temple.

Not long after our return, a friend from my adventure in New Mexico discovered an ancient artifact which seemed to indicate the location of the fourth gateway. After following the clues, we discovered a shapeshifting Cat Person who had come to our world to get help in stemming the tide of corruption in its own world. This was the second world. Not long after returning home, a friend from New Mexico offered an artifact for inspection that ultimately led to the discovery of the fourth gate. This had been used by a shapeshifting creature from the second world who asked our assistance in ridding his home from evil.

By following old Navajo legends and the trail of the jet stone, which had been a prison for a princess, we came into the second world to try and fight off the evil which had devastated the second world. In the second world we battled sorcerers, undead cat creatures, and shapeshifters. We also managed to free the queen of the Cat People from her centuries-long imprisonment and restore her to the throne.

It was she that gave us the scroll we had been translating. The document was written by the sorcerer who was from our world. He'd travelled to the other world on instructions from the Master to seed corruption in that place. We had hoped to learn the location of the fifth gate from the cryptic writing in the document.

As we had stopped evil again and again, we gained confidence that we could face any new threat. With only one gate left to find, our chances seemed to be getting better.

Arianna was an old girlfriend from my schooldays. Though it had been broken off years ago, mostly due to my emotional retardation, we worked together well when fighting evil in the second world and currently as we translated the scroll. We felt nearer to discovering the location of the crystal gate – as it was referred to in the scroll.

The first four gates, the gate of stone, wood, water, and the geode, had been found and were now in our control. This last gate, the crystal gate, was the final link with which we could stop evil from entering our world once and for all. Well that one evil anyway.

I had always believed that evil was not some universal power that manifested or was wrought by a single entity. I thought that evil was simply an idea. An idea of something that goes against the good of the living. Some miasmic darkness which presents as a defect in the personality of the unscrupulous. Though it does stem from many places, evil can present as one mind powerful enough to corrupt all it touches. That was what we faced. So far, we were still alive. Somehow, we were winning.

It was one of the reasons I smiled. There had been many more.

Maria and her romance with Keith had blossomed to the point they were ready to get married. I had the honor of being best man. I imagined that I would make a horrible one.

It also seemed to be that my time with Arianna had been in some ways better than our time together when we dated years ago. I had changed a lot since then. Perhaps I was starting to become someone with a personality. No. That would assume too much.

At any rate, our translations had gone slowly. Though we could often get the words translated correctly, we had problems with the metaphors which were in almost every element of the scroll.

Suppose you were to use one of the amazing translation programs that are available to get the exact word for word translation of one language to another. In some cases, there might not be words that directly translate. In other cases, there was a sort of unwritten element. Context, metaphor, and allegory are much more difficult to interpret.

Without cultural reference and understanding of metaphor, words can sometimes be misleading. It had only been in the past thousand years or more that punctuation has been used to help identify some element of context in western language.

In short, we had a good idea of where to start but information was limited. One thing that stood out was mention of a sort of table like structure in an arid location which struck a note of memory with me. The way it had been described in the scroll made me think of the Gabarnmung rock shelter in Australia. I thought Arianna and I should investigate further.

Between the two of us, we had a great deal of knowledge about symbols and linguistics related to the early aboriginal Australia. Her from her academic studies, and me from the rigorous study my parents had forced upon me.

We concluded it might be possible that some of the information recorded in the rock art at that site might help us in our quest.

We'd spent some days studying the records that had been posted of the art and been somewhat frustrated as it seldom showed the art in context to the surrounding markings. As with so many other records, those that had published the information did so based on what looked interesting as opposed to how it had been presented in the first place. And much was jumbled on top of itself making separation of the symbols difficult.

Arianna was going on the premise that some of the art would be related to other aspects based on location. If two paintings were opposed or in an odd alignment it might mean something different than if they were overlaid or juxtaposed.

Though we thought of the trip as being purely academic, we would need to decide on who to take with us. There had always been danger when we'd gone on these adventures.

Having Been Warned in a Dream

Arianna, Maria, Nick, Conner, Hector, Min, Lucy, Agent Jermyn, and Doris gathered in the library. There was also myself, of course.

Arianna and I had discussed the potential for danger and the need for the most experienced of us to be actively involved in the mission. That she and I took charge of setting the team was not questioned by the others. I think mostly because everyone agreed how the group should be composed.

Maria was exactly as she'd been when I first met her. Her dark hair and pale skin gave a sort of goth caste. The black and white vestments she wore could might have indicated she was either puritan or Amish. Maria's first born, Thomas, was doing well and Aunt Doris had moved into the house to act as nanny. Maria was six months into her second pregnancy. This was precisely the same point as in her first pregnancy when she and I had survived the death of all her family. During that time, she'd shown great reserves of resolve. However, our team had grown since then and the situation warranted her staying at home and acting as a sort of reference library. She could access the family documents and aid us from the safety of the library in which we gathered.

Conner, the heavily muscled ex-marine seemed happy and yet focused. His light hair and deep set blue eyes moved across the room in a combination of study and apprehension. It was as though he were sizing up the team and preparing for a battle. We knew he would not be coming with us though.

Conner would be reticent to leave his pregnant wife and family. We had decided that, if physical defense were needed, we should call upon Nick Wills. Slightly taller than Conner and less heavily built, Nick was an ex-Army Ranger who had become disenchanted with his career. He was Conner's right hand during our adventure in Asia and was as capable as anyone I'd ever met.

We had also come to depend on the insights of Min and Hector. I'd met them in New Mexico and come to think of them as family. Perhaps closer than that. I shared a link with Hector that included twice having shared transitions into the mind of the rift. His insights had proven dependable. Though small framed, he had a reserve of endurance that he carried as a badge of honor. No matter the cost, he would see his duty to the end.

Min was from a family that had, in the past, been protectors of a gate. She'd been trained in martial arts and Asian mysticism. As a fighter, she was unequaled, and as a resource on the ancient practices surrounding the battle against corruption, she was invaluable.

We also included Christine Jermyn. Not for the skills she possessed but because she, as a government agent, might be able to help gain access to some of the places we might want to go. She would also be helpful in getting us out of trouble, should the need arise.

Finally, I had wanted to include Lucy because of her medical background. There might be potential for injury and having someone who had experience with corruption and the battle we faced might be helpful. Also, Hector was her brother. They'd grown up together and it might be difficult to separate them during a dangerous adventure.

Arianna had objected on the grounds that she would not be helpful as either a researcher or as a potential combatant.

Though I agreed in principle, I also realized that I felt a certain obligation toward her. It was because I convinced her husband to become involved in my battle against corruption that he'd been killed, and I felt an obligation to her. She had decided, after much soul searching, to help the cause. If I could, I felt I should, offer her that much. She'd been a real champion during our incursion into the Second World.

In the end my argument was accepted and she'd been invited.

So we gathered. The library seemed to be full for the first time since I had wandered up the stairs with a bottle of merlot two years before. The cast had changed.

Where once was a family that seemed so strange and yet so inviting to me, now sat a family of people that were so different and yet so similar. Min sat where Stevanie had. Maria was in the same chair she'd sat in when I came here two years ago. Lucy sat off to the left in the other chair. Doris sat in a wood harp-backed chair midway between the stairs and the door. Her largish frame blocked access somewhat but her congenial nature brightened the room.

Like before, the men all stood. Nick seemed to have aged. His youthful face had earned a few lines of experience. He stood leaning against the hand rail.

Hector stood next Min. His gaze seemed to shift between me and Min. Hector was a doctor of virology who had recently completed his PhD at UNM. His mind was as sharp as any I knew and he was also a man of action. I loved him for his nature. No matter how bad a situation was, he could find a way to make me smile.

Conner stood next to Maria. There was so much love between the two. It had transcended his death. That is to say, the death of Keith. Now Conner and Keith had been joined into a single mentality inhabiting the body of the ex-marine Conner. Occasionally they would look at each other and even I could feel the earth stop.

Arianna stood next to me near the desk in the center of the room. It was an old oak tilt-up. The chair set in front had been pushed all the way in and was unused by our assembly.

Arianna and I had developed a decent working relationship. Where we had once been lovers, we were now companions of academic pursuit. There had been no hint of romance between us. I suppose that we'd crossed that bridge long ago and had moved on. Our recent reconnection had rekindled the shared love of academics and language but not of each other.

Over the last few months I realized I could anticipate her actions and thoughts somewhat. She seemed to share the skill. Between us, we had not only translated the scroll but arrived at conclusions as to the metaphor and inference based on our combined knowledge. The truth was, she'd done most of the translating.

I might not have mentioned, but she is an eminent linguist. Having written several textbooks and being a professor of language studies made her an unparalleled resource on interpreting the scroll. After her, I was a poor second.

She deferred to me, though, as de facto leader to let them in on what we had discovered.

"I'm glad you all made it," I started. "Arianna and I have made a great deal of progress on the scroll and felt it was time to take action on what we discovered. First, though, I wanted to thank her for getting involved in the struggle.

I know it seems a little late to thank you all but I would like to do that as well."

"Thank you," I said. "I know it seems somehow unnecessary but I felt I should."

"The document is somewhat hazy on several points but it does point to the fact that corruption has been known and battled for at least written history. The one we think might have been Pi-ja-mi-nu or Piyamaradush, seemed to have been involved in spreading corruption not only in our world but was an agent in the second world as well. It could be possible that he had been active in other places as well."

"At any rate, it was his scroll Arianna has been translating. She and I have discussed the possibilities and are confident that a good starting point to search for the fifth gate will be the Australian outback. A few references that indicated a table shaped rock structure with 36 pillars of rough stone decorated with thousands of pictures of the battle between the darkness in the dream and the light of the waking time are mentioned in his scroll."

"I think, based on that description, it might be the Gabarnmung rock shelter. The location is sacred to the aborigines of the area and it is said by their mystics that it's the location where the Mimi communicate with the people. The Mimi are a sort of guardian angel of the Arnhem land Aborigines."

"I think that it is likely that some of the legends of Australian antiquity might be related to the rift. I also think it's worth checking out the table rock structure in person. What I am proposing is, Arianna and I lead a team including Nick, Hector, Min, Lucy, and Agent Jermyn. We go check it out and we take whatever steps needed to continue to pursue the final open gate."

"I want to be clear. Grieta is the rift. The gates are her senses through which she experiences the universe. I would say they are analogues of eyes and ears, so we can use them as a way of seeing through to other gates. Zach and Maria's father proved this and I've used the method with limited success a few times myself."

"I guess it's a good time for questions. Any?" I finished.

"Do you think I'll be enough protection?" asked Nick.

"I don't expect to encounter anything but, for now, I would rather keep the team to a minimum. Between you and Agent Jermyn, I think we should be ok. Anything other than ordinary and Min, Hector, and I will swing into action. Lucy can act as our medic and conscience," I answered.

"What did the scroll say actually?" asked Lucy. "I mean, not just about the Australian rock shelter thing, but in general?"

"It was a personal journal of the one called Piyamaradush," Arianna answered. "In a nutshell it was the ramblings of a power hungry maniac. But it did give us lots of information to work with. First and foremost, a potential location of the gateway. But more than that it told the story of how this person came into contact with corruption and how he had used it to spread evil not only in our world but in the Second World."

"He must have lived in our world in the time of ancient heroic Greece, maybe 1200 to 1350 BCE. He'd been in the Eastern Aegean fighting a war when he encountered some agents of corruption. They led him to Egypt where he used some sort of magic to commune with the master. In the journal, the master is referred to as the last ancient. There was a mention of four old beings that aided humanity in their desire for technology and power. A war arose between these ancient beings and their followers. One side followed the master the other followed the one referred to as the Messa or Begasta. These of course were only agents of higher powers that sought control of all of creation."

"In the end, the followers of the last ancient lost and were banished to darkness. Somehow they managed to find the way to the second world. I think that the master somehow aided them in their exile. There is some difficulty translating because of inconsistent metaphor. I guess I should say it because I don't understand some of the metaphors used. Anyway, Piyamaradush managed to escape exile by finding a passage to the second world."

"From there, the scroll rambles about getting the king to betray his own daughter and using his corruption to influence political affairs. Basically a self-aggrandizing autobiography."

"There are several references to four ancient beings who aided the creatures of light and darkness. After several discussions with Chris, we have come to the conclusion that the being known as 'the Master' is the fourth of these ancients."

"We also think that the second one might be the one called Begotsiti or BegoChiddi by some southwestern Native Americans. The one that helped the first man come to our world."

"If that is the case, then we know that the second ancient was active in helping humanity escape corruption. Or at least escape the effects of it."

"The other ancient beings are unknown. It is possible that there are more than the four mentioned but it seems as though only these four have had any interaction with humanity."

"Grieta is not one of these ancients. After long debates, we both think the rift is a separate entity that has been somewhat aloof from the machinations of these four beings till recently. By recently I mean the last few thousand years on our world."

"There is a great deal of evidence that time flows differently in different worlds. We were active in the second world for what seemed like several weeks. When we returned, only a few hours had passed. Also, Chris tells me that while he and Hector were within the rift during your New Mexico adventure, hours seemed to pass. Yet after exiting the rift, mere seconds had elapsed."

"Anyway, we know that these ancient beings have influenced affairs on our world and the second world. It is safe to say that this ancient conflict might be older than humanity. Who knows what the real cost might have been over the eons. We thought it might be helpful to look for more recent references of the second ancient but there haven't been any we can be sure of except the rather obvious native myths."

"All we can say is that we are still trying to safeguard our world against corruption. For now, that means finding the last of these five primary gateways and locking it against corruption."

"We should probably confer with Grieta again before we leave. She may have other insights about the gate we have missed," Maria added.

I nodded. Maria was chaffing a little about being left out. I knew that she wanted to be on the front line should anything happen. She was the more proficient when it came to spell casting and battling corruption. I considered myself a poor second. I would have to do. Besides, she'd risked and lost so much already. I felt it my place to protect her even when she didn't need it.

Conner would have loved to come on the mission. His knowledge of archeology and anthropology might have been valuable. I knew that he would only go if Maria went. He stayed by her side, a dutiful husband and father. No, I couldn't ask him to leave her. Even if I did, I doubt he would.

In the end, the lack of any further comment or question left us with the last task of consulting Grieta. In the past, we might have gone to the cellar and contacted her through the gate which presented itself as a large crack in an ancient rock face. The tunnel that passed from under the house into the hillside behind it led to what had once been a riverbed. There was no need to go as both Min and I protected a half of the geode we'd secured in New Mexico.

The geode had been protected by my parents previously. During a small battle with a group of cultists, the geode had been split. Each half now had the full power of the whole as well as the unique connection allowing instant transfer from one to the other. Both halves were connected by a permanent gate. This gate could be used to traverse to another world or to simply the other half. We had accidentally used that ability when Hector and I drove corrupting mentalities from Grieta.

My half of the geode was stored in a glass enclosure next to the Dagger of Thane which stood upon the mantle in the sitting room downstairs. Min kept her half stored in a family vault in California under the watchful eye of her grandfather.

We decided to reconvene in the lounge downstairs. As each person stepped past me I nodded and smiled. When Maria passed I motioned for her to wait. I had an important question to ask and I knew that she might be the only one who would understand the context.

Conner smiled as he noticed my action and said in a quiet voice that he would keep the company entertained till we joined them.

Once the room was empty, I asked my question.

"Maria, I was wondering.... You felt how much power we were able to draw from the second world itself for our spells. I have been thinking. The energy we felt as the spells were cast seemed to have a kind of emotional charge. Do you think it is possible that we could use our own emotional state as a way of creating power?"

The basic construct of a spell was multipart. In the simplest terms, it might be equated to a sentence. You needed a noun and a verb to create the basic "he goes" or "she sits." More complex spells would be like complex sentences such as "he goes slowly northward." Even more complex sentence construction might describe walking or riding a bike.

The point is that you need purpose and power to create any spell effect. The purpose could be equivalent to the noun. The power would be the verb. You need both to make the thought complete. While in the world of the cat people we found that energy was abundant. We could create and cast spells by drawing upon the residual energy of the world.

On earth there is no wellspring of energy. We must create the empowering part of the spell mechanically. I had begun theorizing that it might be possible to energize a spell with emotions. By creating a heightened emotional state, then processing the spell components, we might be able to add additional power to the spell effect.

"The old books seem to indicate that you can, but there is a danger," Maria agreed. "Using emotional energy drains your life force, stealing your essence for the spell. You will recover slowly. If you use too much, or use it incorrectly, you might permanently weaken yourself. You could even die if you don't do it right."

“Oh, I thought I was making a new discovery with this. You say it has been recorded in the family journals?” I asked.

“Actually, Jamas had researched the topic pretty thoroughly. I played with the idea some but was afraid to pursue it too far due to the dangers inherent in application. Since we returned from the second world I have given the subject more thought, though. I think with some practice it could be a viable technique,” she replied.

“Thanks. I’ll give it some thought.” I shrugged and followed her downstairs.

Lessons from the Past

We gathered around a small table on which sat the geode. I gazed at its white crystal inner surfaces and spoke the Etruscan chant activating the lens.

"Let me see through you. This metal is the same as your metal and they are in harmony. I can see through the mirror I create."

Instantly a feeling of calm and joy came over me. I felt the presence of Grieta. Her mind was close. Above the geode, a small reflection of the crack in the cellar wall hovered. It was from here that I felt the mind of the rift open up to us.

"You come to speak to me again my friends," the voice was as much in our minds as it was a sound issuing from the glowing ribbon that surrounded the image of the rift.

"What is it that you wish to ask? I know that there is something pressing you into action. I can sense it in all of your thoughts."

"We have translated the scroll and have decided to check out some sites in Australia. But we have a few things we need more clarity on. I was hoping you could help." I spoke for all of us. I had the best relationship with the rift and though it was never discussed, I knew I would be the one talking for the group.

"You would know of the four?" Grieta asked.

"Please?" I replied.

"These four are ancient beings older than humanity. They are from the early universe. Like me, they became aware over the eons. They were once simply mentalities without form. Unlike me they were bound to singularity. That is to say they are not connected to the greater universe but bound to a single place in space-time. Though they could move through space, they also occupy space, where as I do neither. They are younger that me but older than your world."

"As they drifted through the universe, they watched the planets and stars being born, and in time they observed the beginnings of life. Later still, they became aware of the one quality that evolved life has that they did not possess. The ability to create is unique to creatures that can imagine. The greater the imagination, the more diverse the creation. Some creatures can only effect change for themselves such as shifting forms like the people of the second world."

"Humans have a very unique ability to create freely. Though you lack the requisite power to create, you may borrow power from your surroundings and effect change in your world. This can be mechanically with tools and machines or mentally through shear will and emotion."

"The ancient beings cannot do this. One of them began to test the limits of human creation by teaching people how to bend power to their will. People began to create great things, and terrible things."

"When a person creates something good, the action generates a power of life and light. This energy is felt as joy and comfort in the world."

"When a person creates evil, there is a small release of dark energy. This energy is the thing you refer to as corruption. It is an infection that spreads and devours. Though you may resist its influence, it will either empower you or destroy you."

"Corruption is a power source that can be used for only destruction. So unreleased in your body, it destroys the host. In your case, Chris, it will devour you eventually." She paused.

A question jumped out of my mouth before I could think to stop it. "You slowed the corruption before, can it be cured somehow?" I asked. I was getting us off topic and I knew how selfish I was being but I couldn't stop myself.

"Time is an element of life. I simply slowed time temporarily or really I slowed the effect of time on your cells. But eventually time catches up. I did what I could but there is no other way to slow the effect of corruption other than end the source of corruption. As much as it sounds wonderful to do, the source of corruption is humanity."

The world stopped. Thousands of comments and questions ran through my mind all at once. I could feel the minds of the others racing to understand the implication of the revelation. It was Hector that provided the question.

“What about the Master and all that? How does he fit into this? Isn’t he the one that spreads corruption?”

“You are right that the one called the Master spreads corruption. Indeed, it is seeded in the new world by the minions of the Master. But corruption was created by humanity. It is the ash left over when evil is done. Like the charred remains after a forest fire. The Master is one of the four ancient minds,” Grieta continued.

“One of the others taught people to create. That one simply wanted to know the limit of power in evolved creatures. Once it had discovered the terrible consequences of using this power, he warned the other ancient beings. The one called the Master realized the threat and became convinced that controlling corruption was the only way to safeguard its own existence.”

“It went to the world of men and took the form of a creature of legend. There it incited war and famine. Destruction of humanity was nearly assured. But the first ancient who had spent time with humanity, teaching and advising and guiding the course of history, had come to cherish humanity for the potential good that might be done.”

"The Teacher found a new world free of corruption that also had very little available power for creation. He began to lead people there by teaching them about the gateways through me. It was hoped that in this new world people could learn to live peacefully. That world was already populated by other humans who were the same as those from the first world. He helped create colonies where the native people and the new people could live together harmoniously."

"Corruption followed, though. It is an undying seed that once created could not be forgotten. Without the power to grow freely, corruption would need help from the Master."

"The Master learned that people had escaped their own world and been saved on another. It searched and searched for this other world. I was unaware of its plan and helped for a time. For that, I am ashamed. Once I realized what it wanted, I did my best to close the gates to its use. By then, thousands of worlds had come under its control. It found it could send the minds of its servants through into host creatures. This is a side effect of crossing the rift."

"Perhaps a side effect isn't the right phrase. It is one effect of crossing the rift. A mind travels better than a body. Mentalities of great will can force themselves into host bodies through the contact plane known as a gateway."

“Thus began the slow enslavement of thousands of worlds. I could only slow their progress within the rift. But I was powerless to act outside of this domain. Until recently when I found I could act by transmitting my power through into host bodies like that of Conner. I could absorb the consciousness of those that were worthy and by the same mechanic that the Master spread corruption, I could spread my influence.”

“What of the other ancients? You said there were four?” I asked.

“There were in fact many more than just four. These four travelled together and acted as companions for a time. The one who taught, the master, one who observed, and the last which seemed more interested in staying out of the machinations of the others. I think that the last one acted as a sort of go between. When any of the others disagreed about something, the last ancient being would help them resolve their differences.”

“For a long time, this worked. However, once the Master began to use corruption to enhance its own power instead of simply protecting the old ones from potentially dangerous peoples, the entire group split and went their separate ways.”

“The being that was helping humanity and the Master began a long slow battle for the lives and future of all the evolved beings in the universe.”

I thought about the native legend and wondered if the one helping humanity was called Begotsidi in Navajo and Hopi myths.

"You are right Chris," Grieta had heard my mental question. "That one was called Begotsidi among other names. From now on, to help in telling the history, I will use that name," she continued.

"Some time ago the Master began to experiment. Was it possible for an ancient being to die, or to have their existence end? In order to test the theory, it devoured the life force of several of the ancients including Begotsidi. This ended the long battle between the old companions."

"The Master hoped that this would also speed the end of humanity, but humanity has a resilience. It also has strength that the master could not understand or predict. Humans possess both highly imaginative minds and highly emotional spirits. This gives them an unparalleled power. Not even the ancients can defeat that combination. So the Master seeks to subvert that Strength by giving humanity a reason to spread its own corruption: Power over others."

"Then there is a way to destroy the Master?" I asked. "How?"

A long pause told me that Grieta was reticent about the answer. I knew that it was something that needed doing if we were to finally win out against the evil that we faced. I was also beginning to be aware that we were the source of corruption and therefore the originators of the reason why this evil existed.

"There are few ways to do this but most lead to more corruption being created. For all the evil the Master has sown in the universe, it is part of the beginnings of the universe and therefore intrinsic to it. Destruction creates corruption, even destruction of evil. For it to work without creating an overwhelming tide of corruption, an equal sacrifice of power must be made. I cannot say more than this."

As Grieta closed her contact with us, the pang of loss and sadness filled my heart. My vision was blurred by tears. I felt weak. I also realized a great shame. Knowing that humanity was responsible for the evil that we now faced made it more imperative that we succeed. If only to make up for the damage that had been done. If only to stem the tide.

The Outback

The predawn air was dry. I could feel the faint breeze rustle against the side of the large tent in which I slept. My dreams of late had been of death. My death. In the dreams I would die, coughing, gasping for air. I would wake up soaked and tired. I felt my end was coming. I must finish my task before my time was over.

I crawled from my sleeping bag and stood slowly. A tingle in my throat made me gasp at the impending wrack of coughing I knew would follow. I took a deep breath and began my exercise. The slow meaningful tai chi-like movement allowed me to stifle the urge to cough. The deep, even breathing that was an integral part of the form calmed my mind and allowed me to think clearly again.

Death was an enemy I knew well. I'd seen the shadowed form take many friends. After the suffering and pain of the last two years, I felt as though I could welcome the end. If only I could know for sure that my world would be safe from the corruption that it faced. For now, I felt I could be content if that last gateway was closed.

The first step was to investigate the stone table rock formation nearby. It stood on land reserved for the aboriginal people of the area. We had been allowed to camp a little over a mile away. Concern over the spirits that guarded the place caused the elders to insist on some distance between our camp and the site itself.

We waited for an old woman who acted as a tour guide and a sort of village storyteller to arrive. She would take us to the site and give us the full tour. I wondered what she would think when she realized our true motivation for journeying here.

Many people had taken us for fanatics or charlatans. The world as a whole was not really interested in chasing stories of evil from another world. As entertainment it played well, but the conspiracy theory aspect of our work was laughed at.

People simply didn't want to believe that something could topple their worldview. Not something like this anyway. It might have been easier if it were an invasion from space.

After the long slow meditation of motion and breathing, I sat at the fold up table centered near our fire pit. Bacon and eggs were offered as breakfast, cooked by Nick.

I'd insisted that there be no other members of the team other than the few I'd chosen. Our last endeavor in southeast Asia had left a bad taste in my mouth and I only wanted people I could trust in the camp. Nick had agreed and thus we hired no porters or camp cooks. It was just the few of us having to do for ourselves.

A large SUV stood to one side of the camp. We'd used this to cross the couple of hundred kilometers from Darwin to the Gabarnmung rock shelter. Though there was an old air strip less than two miles away, we were unwilling to be in the wilds of the Northern Territory without a vehicle.

Four tents stood in a semicircle. The one on the north end housed our supplies and was set up as a sort of headquarters. The next was reserved for Hector and Min. Mine stood south of the center. I shared it with Nick. Arianna, Lucy, and Agent Jermyn used the southern-most tent.

Everyone had finished breakfast except me. They'd left several strips of bacon and four over medium eggs. Without asking, I took them all. As I ate, I tried to ignore the doubts that continued to creep into my mind.

I hadn't been feeling very well lately. Even my complexion seemed pale and sallow. The skin of my face seemed to sag more. Deep lines of either worry or age creased my countenance. The glittery silver and blue indications of corruption in my body made my eyes glow in a dark and sinister reflection.

I'd come to know more about the evil that we faced than almost anyone ever had. With the exception of Maria, I was the only real authority I knew of on the evil we faced. I wondered at the legacy I would leave when I finally succumbed to the disease that slowly devoured me.

These troubled thoughts were interrupted as I heard the distant approach of a vehicle on the nearby dirt road. Looking west, I could see a cloud of dust above the line of thorny underbrush and eucalyptus trees. That must be our guide.

The jeep slid to a halt only a few yards from the southernmost tent. Before the sound of the engine died, a short, round woman leapt from the driver's seat and landed catlike on her feet. She was talking to herself as she strode toward the group now gathered at the table. Though rather short in stature, she seemed to command our attention as she approached. Her light blue, flower-patterned dress clung closely to her rotund figure. The heavy brown boots she wore seemed out of place.

Her name was Martha. She informed us she'd been the tribal storyteller since her grandfather had passed the tradition on to her. As a child, she'd learned all the legends of her people. Now at the age of seventy she was one of the few remaining people that knew the old history of the family, passed on orally. "You may not write down what I tell you. That would offend the ancestors. So please remember all I say," she offered.

I introduced our team to her and asked her to tell us the history of the rock formation we were investigating. As we walked the mile southward to our destination, she told us of the place and its long history.

So that I don't break the rules she set down, I'll paraphrase the story she told, leaving out the hyperbole and focusing on the elements that were pertinent to our investigation.

The story seemed to start with a being named Banaitja. This one either settled the people in the northern territory or as some legends ascribe, created the people by pulling them from the clay. The legend was given to Martha's great grandfather in a dreaming.

It is said that the people of Australia were first brought here over water during a dreaming. In one version of the story, there had been fighting among the people that led to many leaving their old home and seeking a new land where they could live in peace. Banaitja showed them the passage through which they could come into the lands of peace.

This being then taught them how they could find all the things they needed in the dreaming. The dreaming is a spiritual state only achieved during a dream. A person could commune with their ancestors or the Banaitja. Secrets of the land and of a spiritual nature would be told only to those worthy of the dreaming. The tale of the land was written on the walls and ceiling of the Gabarnmung shelter by generations of those people who could achieve the dreaming. Only they could pass it forward to the next generation.

As I listened, a familiar note seemed to ring. The being known as Banaitja seemed a lot like Begotsidi of the Navajo legend. I wondered if they might have been the same being.

By understanding the dreaming, a creature known as the rainbow serpent reminded the people of their connection to the land and the need to know their place in the greater world, not as above it but as part of it.

When a person acted against the land, the serpent would remind them by stopping the rain or poisoning the wildlife that the people hunted. In this way, the people always understood the way to live on the land as a part of the world.

We came into sight of the terrace of stone that stood out above the stark scrub. Even from a distance I could see the thousands of paintings in brilliant red and yellow covering almost every surface. I found that I had stopped breathing on the exhale in astonishment and forced air into my lungs. A small cough escaped as I breathed out.

Martha continued to tell of the history and legend surrounding the place. This was a place where the elders of the people would come to dream. Here the Mimi would show people secrets and signs. They might teach the people a new skill such as how to make a spear or a new fish hook. Or they would warn the people of danger or disaster that must be avoided.

Now we were only a few dozen yards from the cave-like structure and Martha fell silent. I heard her breathing in an odd, uneven pattern. Her head was bowed and her arms seemed to slowly spread from her sides.

She told us that the Mimi were here and they would like us to come see the work of the old ones.

We cautiously moved under the stone terrace and stared in wonder at the spirals and lines that made up many of the figures. Here a kangaroo, there a lizard, many snakes and even the occasional koala spread above us. People engaged in everything from hunting to giving birth were presented as unique objects of art painted over sixty thousand years of human occupation.

I say sixty thousand because I read that early dating places humanity in this part of the world almost as far back as that. The wonder of it was this would have been nearly thirty-five thousand years before people came into North America.

Though time is somewhat relative in the rift, Banaitja would have been actively helping people escape evil long before Begotsidi led the migration that ended with ancestors of the Navajo finding their way to the Southwest. If they were the same being, then he was active in human affairs for all of human history.

As Martha's tour wound its way through the maze of columns, Arianna and I looked for clues in the paintings that might help reveal the location of the gate. Occasionally she would see something that looked promising and motion for me to come over.

I have a pretty good memory so I filed the position and content of each potential clue into my mind and moved on. There were several paintings that seemed to indicate the Mimi beings teaching people new skills or divulging secrets about the world. One of these caught my eye.

It depicted a black painted Mimi standing over a group of people. It's long thin arms seemed twisted in unnatural ways. The twin eyes were surrounded by bands of red and white. Around its head was a halo of red ocher interrupted by black irregular lines. The people and the Mimi were separated by lines which indicated a river. Instead of offering a lesson, it seemed to stand guard over a crack in the rock which had been chiseled roughly behind the being.

It was the shape of the opening in the rock that caught my attention. The angle and edges were very reminiscent of the gateway through which a person accessed the rift.

In every instance where I'd come across a gateway, the familiar geometry was the same. A crack that went from lower left toward upper right at an angle slightly higher than 45 degrees. At the top and bottom, the crack came together but near the middle it widened like an opening into the unknown. Light spilled from the crack in the form of yellow lines. The figure of the Mimi was not the gentle teacher but took a sinister form that seemed to indicate an inherent danger to the people pictured nearby. I asked Martha to tell me about the painting. Her reply was that not all Mimi are good. Some come from the cracks with evil in them.

From the position and composition of the art I thought that it must be somewhat newer than most of the rest. A few mental calculations and I got a timeframe of maybe six to four thousand years BCE. A small clue that I'd almost missed was in the form of the river which ran between the people and the Mimi.

The upper section of the river seemed to be a delta. Along its length there were several elements which looked like interruptions or maybe rapids. Perhaps they indicated cataracts. Along the river, at intervals, tall thickets of reeds stood. I'd seen these depictions before, on the walls of a temple in Egypt. We had our next clue.

Dark Ones

That night I'd retired to my tent. In my mind I continued to review the events of the day. The clue that led to Egypt was tentative at best. I thought it might be a good time to consult the charm of seeing.

The small crystal stone in a hoop was given to me by the Drakson family two years ago. It has the ability to answer a well phrased question by changing temperature. Slight changes might signal either a positive or negative response. A large change in the crystal might indicate danger or worse.

I'd gotten better over the time I'd owned it in asking the right questions and interpreting the responses. Still, it was always right. The challenge was in understanding the answer.

I thought for I while and decided on the simplest form of question I could. "Should we travel to Egypt next?" The slight warming gave me a confident positive. That was settled then as soon as we got into range of cell service, I'd call Maria and have her arrange for our trip.

For some time, my mind wandered but eventually I slept.

Dreams have meaning. They can sometimes reveal to us things our conscious mind is unable to understand. Dreams are also an expression of possible futures. We can occasionally put together seemingly unrelated clues that allow us to dream of a possible outcome. This is sometimes felt as a sort of déjà vu. In many ways our subconscious mind is very powerful.

The mist was light and soft. Many of my dreams began as a parting of the mist and this one was true to form.

The scene, revealed in my dream, was of a scrub land. Scraggly grasses and the occasional thorny bush covered the light brown, sandy soil. Streaks of reddish clay marbled the sandstone outcroppings. Atop a small rounded stone squatted a black figure.

It was a man. Though clothed only in a red sash that wound around his waist and looped over his shoulder, he seemed unconcerned about the rainclouds gathering overhead. His grey streaked hair was bound in a top knot with the same red cloth. Craggy features indicated he must be very old.

"Closer," said the slightly high pitched voice. "I would like to see who you are."

I took a few steps toward him and stopped. I could see his eyes now. They almost glowed. A white slash of pigment had been wiped across his forehead.

"That's close enough," he said. His accent was defiantly aboriginal. There was a slight twang to his words that made me feel uneasy. "So why you comin' here?" he asked.

"I don't know," I responded. "I think I am supposed to find out something. Maybe to ask you about the evil?" I mused.

"You wanna' know about the evil?" he seemed indignant. "Ok, I'll tell then. You ain't gonna like what I say."

"Well, that hasn't stopped me before. I'm just trying to get this all sorted out," I said. "Besides, this is just a dream so what you say might just be my mind interpreting things I already know."

"A dream in this place is not just a dream. When you are in the dreaming you can see the world as it is, or as it should be, or as it will be if you fail to act right. So if I tell you, then you still gotta figure out what to do," he replied.

"Fair enough. I will keep that in mind."

"The evil is not what you think. It is dark and horrible, true. But it will offer power, strength. Maybe even take away the darkness in you. It can, you know. It can control what you call corruption and draw it out of you and use it for its own needs. You can't be cured because you are human. But the stuff in you can be drawn out. If you give in to what it wants."

"What is it that it wants?" I asked. I already knew the answer.

“It wants to continue existing. But it knows that people have the power to stop it. People can create and they can destroy. You help it out and it will make sure you live. It only wants to make sure of its own living,” he said.

“And if I refuse?”

“You are dying anyway. Maybe it will end your suffering by making you die quick. Maybe it will kill all your friends too. End their suffering. It seems an easy trade.”

“Why are you helping it. Who are you anyway?” I insisted.

“I’m your own mind. I am you. I am that part of you that has embraced corruption. I’m the thing that is killing you.”

“Thanks for taking things so slow,” my sarcasm was not lost. “You are giving me time to finish what I started.”

“Your threat is meaningless. The Master will win. Time is our ally. You have so little of that left.” A slight laugh escaped him with the taunt.

In the distance I heard a sound. At first it was a low short rumble. Then it returned louder and longer. The next burst of sound caused me to start. I was awake.

I heard the sound again. To my now awake ears it seemed like an angry person yelling. “Arrrggghhh!!!!”

The voice nearly unnerved me somehow, like a scream of rage charged with insanity.

Struggling to my feet, I realized that Nick was also awake. He reached for his handgun which hung in its holster from a belt placed on the floor between us. In a single motion he drew and pulled the hammer back. His thumb slipped the safety to the fire position.

I reached forward and unzipped the door of the tent while he stayed to one side ready in case of need.

Once open, he stepped forward out of the tent and swept his weapon left and right. Then he motioned for me to follow. Another scream erupted to our left. It seemed to be nearer than before.

Nick moved his aim in the direction of the sound and moved forward with even and sure steps. I fell in behind and to the right. My mind raced through several spells I had woven in to my garments. Though they were all effective against creatures of corruption, I knew that the potential drain on my personal energy would be considerable.

I had one other potential weapon, my corruption sight. This was granted me when I'd destroyed that first creature in the Drakson family home. I'd been covered in the glittery dust of the creature and breathed it in. It got into my eyes and throat. It gave me the ability to see creatures of corruption by simply focusing. This ability comes at a price. If I use the power, corruption moves freely though me hastening my eventual death.

I felt that I should risk it now in order to understand what we faced.

As my sight became attuned to corruption I could see the glittery emanation of dark silver and red some thirty feet in the scrub. The shape was roughly human and though still distant, I could tell that the creature was a living being. When corrupted, the living give off a much higher level of glittery darkness than a corrupted corpse.

Nick moved to the left slightly to avoid a bush. As he did so, I moved to the right of the bush hoping that we could keep the creature in either of our field of vision.

I heard the sounds of the rest of the camp waking and moving behind us. A soft pad of feet accompanied by a much louder crashing told me that Min and Hector had come up to my right offering a longer skirmish line.

A soft laughing cackle came from the creature ahead. I felt I'd heard it before. Though usually dependable, the memory escaped me. Where had I heard that laugh before?

The being was standing in what seemed to be an open area now only twenty yards ahead. Its legs spread wide, and its arms hung in the shape of long hooks to its sides. It seemed slightly hunched.

"There you are," it laughed. "I have you finally. This time on my own terms." The harsh scratchy voice forced open the memory of Seattle.

In the underground tunnels that crisscrossed the older section of the city, we had come across this evil being. We chased it from the tunnels but hadn't been able to destroy it. It must have been waiting for the best chance to attack. Now nearly a year and a half later it chose the time to strike.

Nick responded by shooting twice into its chest.

The thing looked down at the holes as glittery dust fell gently from the injury. It then looked at Nick with a smile and drew and fired its old style revolver. There was no loud bang. A spark of fire erupted from the barrel and flew at Nick in a wobbly path. I rapidly unloosed a shield spell which barely deflected the projectile.

Min snapped open a yellow and red metal fan and sprinted forward while Hector fired his chrome handgun.

Hector's bullet ripped into the creature just above the right collar, opening a jagged hole that exploded in a shower of corruption.

The thing fell back as Min came forward and launched a front kick into its midsection followed by a vicious slash with the bladed metal ends of her fan.

Hector refrained from further shots in fear of hitting his wife. Nick fell back a few steps to let Min do her work. I moved forward in hopes that I might be able to help her.

The creature had recovered from the initial attack and was using his revolver as a club. He swung it in large arcs that Min was able to easily avoid.

She stabbed at it with kicks and punches as well as slashed and jabbed with her fan. More often than not her attacks connected, opening larger wounds in the thing. By now its face and chest were glowing from a dozen injuries oozing dark corruption.

Seeing that the tide had turned against it, the creature seemed to become more desperate. Attacks were more daring but still not connecting. Then, as an opening presented itself, it fired its pistol point blank into Min. She jerked back as Hector yelled "NO!!"

Hector shot recklessly at the thing. It fell back with each impact. By the time six rounds had connected, it was lying lifeless, draped over a thorny bush. Hector continued to fire another several rounds before his anger and fear for his wife caused him to drop his weapon and rush to her side.

He rolled her over and lifted her into his lap. Looking down at her he could see the signs of corruption beginning to move through her. Her eyes glittered silver and red. There was no open wound, only a large red welt that seemed edged in silver blue. The effect of this creature's weapon was to rapidly corrupt a host, allowing the thing control over the possessed body.

"Get her to Lucy. Quick!" I shouted. We raced back to the camp knowing that we had a limited time before corruption might take control of Min.

Laying her on a cot, Hector stood back, offering Lucy room to do her work.

Lucy had been studying corruption and working her way through the medical journals left by the Drakson family. As a family of doctors going back to the time before the revolution, they'd been studying the medical effects of corruption for centuries. Lucy was an ER nurse so she'd been able to assimilate the information quickly.

She'd also spent some time with Min's uncle in Seattle. He understood the method of removing the seed of corruption which, in the case of the gunfighter, was a small stone. The bullet which had been infused with corruption and was meant to infiltrate the host with corrupting influence.

It was several hours work to remove the bullet. Because the location was primitive, Lucy performed the requisite surgery without the use of modern tools other than those available in her portable medical kit.

I'd watched Min's uncle perform a removal without surgery. He'd used mystical techniques to draw the stone out.

Lucy used modern surgical techniques with added metaphysical elements she'd learned from Thomas Drakson's journals. The stone was small and had nestled in Min's hip. The wound was only about an inch deep so it posed no physical threat to her once stitched. The effect was the same in the end. Min was freed from corruption though she would take some time to heal. I softly added a healing spell of my own hoping that it might speed her recovery.

The next morning, we returned to Darwin by way of the long winding road. Min insisted she didn't need to go to the hospital so we returned to our hotel to plan the next leg of our journey.

Jamas and Kayle

With Min safe, my mind wandered back to the conversation Maria and I had before I left. The nature of magic and power seemed to loom over all of our interaction with corruption and the rift itself. The revelation that corruption was a human invention bothered me some. Especially when I thought of its slow effect on me. I really wanted to know more.

Maria's sister Jamas had written several journals of her own discoveries on the nature of evil. I'd borrowed the last journal that she had been writing, in hoping to understand some of her work on the subject. This seemed like a great opportunity to do research.

This particular volume started as she was travelling all over Asia. She began by chronicling her stay at an old temple in Hunan. There she learned several internal martial arts methods and worked on controlling her emotions.

One of the styles she studied included a philosophy about the useful application of emotion during martial exercises as a method of empowering the artist's actions.

By emoting calm, a person could create a positive defense. By expressing anger at the right moment a person could add power to an attack. By expressing love, a person could endure pain. Each emotion was useful in a variety of ways.

Jamas studied and meditated for more than a year and a half before returning to California where she met up with Kayle to help him work out a problem he'd uncovered at a bay area university.

Kayle parked his older pickup in the arrivals lane. Jamas stood a few feet back from the curb. Her dark olive skin and lean frame seemed almost at odds with that of her brother. She wore the traditional family colors but cut in a more athletic pattern to allow freedom of movement. At her feet, two small pieces of luggage contained all she needed. She'd always been a light traveler, and her requirements were minimal.

Kayle jumped out and swung around the truck in easy rapid motions. His large muscular frame carried him with a grace that seemed more suited to a dancer than an athlete of his size.

The hug of affection the siblings shared showed a deep connection. As twins, they'd been very close growing up. The few years they'd been separated did in fact make their hearts grow fonder.

Since finishing college, Jamas had been on a personal journey, travelling the orient and studying a variety of martial arts styles. She'd also visited several families involved in the battle against corruption and learned many of their beliefs and techniques. She'd only returned to aid Kayle in his own investigations.

Kayle was working on his masters in evolutionary biology. Though he had a full athletic scholarship, in three years he'd finished his undergrad work. With another year of eligibility, he pursued the next level of his education.

During his research he'd been shown that humanity had evolved from several lines of prehumen descendants. Though many had been identified as species such as Homo Erectus and Denisovan, there were at least three that had as yet not been identified.

Kayle had been working on the theory that life evolves in similar ways in similar conditions. This was an extension of the parallel evolution ideas that had been presented in the early days of the science. His work was an extension that included not simply similar environments but also identical worlds. His work would never be published for the outside world but it could enhance the family understanding of the rift and its purpose.

Jamas tossed her bags in the bed of the truck and climbed in. Kayle pulled away and started down the ramp that would lead to the highway and back toward the city. The distant light glittered brightly in the early morning darkness.

"Thanks for coming," Kayle said with a smile. "I thought this was more up your alley than mine."

"You have a mystery that you can't solve and decided I was a better candidate as chief investigator?" Jamas asked.

"Well, in the interest of fair competition, I felt I should bring you in on it," Kayle responded. "You would have hated to be left out of this one."

The two had similar competitive spirits. Throughout their childhood they competed in pretty much every athletic endeavor. Often that spilled over into the academic. By bringing Jamas in on his own investigation, Kayle was reinstituting the sibling rivalry.

At some point a series of rules would be set down so that each would be on equal footing. Competition needed organization. Rules ensured that each participant was evaluated in a fair and unbiased way. Rules for action and a clear set of goals were required in order to frame the activity in a way that could engage each competitor.

Since Kayle had called her, he would create the framework of the competition. Normally it would give him the advantage. Kayle was the ultimate sportsman though. He would ensure that Jamas had an equal chance in the investigation that was coming.

Kayle had an apartment near campus. The one bedroom edifice was expensive but he enjoyed his privacy and, as a graduate student athlete, he was allowed the indulgence.

Jamas was set up on the couch. After her shower, they talked for a while to catch up. By 3:00 AM they retired.

In the morning, the two spoke over breakfast. Kayle laid out his plan. Then he set the rules.

"You are firstly a martial artist but your degree is in oriental studies," he began. "I've come across several things which seem to support my theories. There are however quite a few inconsistencies in practical application. For instance, I've identified several specific genetic markers whose origin I cannot discover. These have been introduced maybe a half dozen times in unrelated or isolated parts of the world. The most recent seems to have been around fifteen hundred years ago in the southwest. The earliest might be fifty-five thousand years ago in Australia."

"I'm not a biologist," Jamas responded. "How can I possibly help with your study?"

"First, this isn't a biology study. I'll explain in a minute. Second, you are uniquely qualified to help. Of all of the family, you are the only one that genetically expressed our native American heritage in a significant way. Those markers are in all of the family but did not express except in you. That is of course part of the nature of genetics."

"Each of us in the family has unique talents and skills. These are perfected by practice but ingrained in our basic makeup. Certainly nurture and nature both play a part. The basic postulation is, how do people who are genetically so very similar and live in essentially the same state of nurture, end up being so unique? Is there some depth of the basic human genome that might be responsible for the individual diversity? Is it simply that some small percentage of genetic divergence means so much in terms of the final disposition of the individual?"

"Still not following," Jamas interrupted. "What are you getting at?"

"In a minute," Kayle replied. "Here is the thing. You and I are twins. We have as much in common as any of those in the family and yet we still are very divergent in so many ways. Those three things, genetics, nurture, and our individual experience makes us who we are."

"What if there is another element to that?" he asked. "What if destiny or fate also paves the way for our potentials to be realized? What if, as so many theologians insist, there is a predetermined, non-genetic mechanism involved?"

"How could you possibly test for that?" Jamas asked. "What metric could you use to even qualify a person's predetermination for a personality type?"

"That is the question," he said in an excited tone. The smile told Jamas he was about to get to the point.

“I met someone,” Kayle began.

“You think it’s destiny to fall for that person?” Jamas smiled.

“No. Not that,” he continued. “This woman came in for one of the genetic studies. I took the sample and was about to usher her out when she said something that gave me a start. She told me that I should get my twin and come to see her. She gave me her address and insisted that she could shed some light on our family business.”

“At first I was taken back. Then she told me that it would be our fate to die soon. She said she could see that much. Perhaps together we might be able to avoid the death that was coming,” his smile widened.

“Of course I thought she was pulling my leg. The more I thought about it the more I felt that if it were even slightly possible that she might be right, I wanted to take the precaution. If I could prevent your death, then I should. But more than that I began to think in terms of fate. I’m sure that Zach would have come up with some really pretty way of metaphorizing the idea. For me, I felt that this might provide an opportunity to study why someone believes in predetermination.”

“Not strictly speaking my field. Really more Zach’s. At any rate, I began to put my theory to the problem. Genetic propensity, nurture, experience, or fate might be a determinant in our deaths that could be predicted by a person that neither you nor I'd ever met."

"Ok. You framed the problem. How do we prove any of what you said? I mean, are we trying to give some kind of percentage of each to categorize the potential influence it might have or simply trying to prove that fate is a real thing?" she asked.

"In our family business, we sort of assume fate as a given. But, is what this person says real? That we will die soon is such an ominous thing to have hanging. It brings out the other side of the question which is maybe more pertinent. Having been warned of our fate, can we change it?" Kayle asked.

"Too many questions for a single study I think," Jamas responded. "Our real goal is simply: does this person believe in fate and how do they get their information?"

"We could start by simply listening. After that we can decide if it is worth pursuing," Kayle continued.

"If it were anyone else I would have been angry for bringing me all this way. As it is, I felt the need to go home. After we are done here, that's what I intend to do. You always do bring me the best questions Kayle."

They arranged to meet the seer later that evening in her own home. She lived on a steep street in the heart of the city. The house was a tall but narrow three story affair.

Its clapboard siding was white but the accent elements were of a dark brown. A large single round window centered the upmost floor. The small front yard was covered in what looked like AstroTurf. The drought had taken its toll on landscaping in recent years.

Jamas paid the cab and followed her brother to the tall six panel door. The upper four panels contained frosted glass while the larger lower two panels were dark mahogany stained wood. The framing of the door was of a slightly lighter wood. Kayle used the knocker centered in the cross of the upper four panels.

The sound of footsteps indicated that the home was largely uncarpeted. The sound of heels on the hardwood floors rapped out a staccato that slowly increased till the door swung open.

A thin woman in her early fifties smiled at the siblings. Without a word she motioned them into her home. Her footsteps were now joined by the softer clap made from the soft athletic shoes of the pair.

Jamas inspected the woman. She was medium height and slightly built. She wore a somewhat modern sundress but it was obviously not ironed. The wrinkles also indicated she probably didn't hang the dress but had tossed it haphazardly into a drawer. Her shoes were simple black heals. Though they added an inch of height, she was still not imposing. Her light brown frizzled hair had begun to grey.

As they entered the parlor at the back of the house, the woman asked them to sit. Several antique chairs and a sofa stood in careful disarray. Two cats curled against each other in a pet bed near a fireplace that had been converted to gas. Additional warmth radiated through the windows at the back which faced the setting sun. This made the house quite warm. The siblings both felt comfortable and welcome.

“I was hoping you could make it here. It’s not long coming. And when I met you at that science thing I knew it was you who I’d seen.” She seemed eager to get the conversation rolling.

“This is your sister then.” A statement, not a question. “She is just like I imagined from my vision.”

“Vision?” Kayle asked.

“Dream really,” she informed him. “But when they are vision dreams, that’s what I call them, they always seem deeper, more deliberate. At any rate, I write those ones down. Or at least as much as I can remember. They fade quickly. Like all dreams I guess.”

“What can you tell us about the vision?” Jamas was always eager to get to the point.

“Simply that someone who was loved more than anything will kill you. And someone you never met will free you.”

"That's it?" Jamas was not impressed.

"No, that's not it," the woman smiled. "I wrote it down. It's my scratching so you probably can't read it. I'll tell you what it says."

"The dream took me to a house covered in words from the past. Inside the six brothers and sisters began to die after the stranger came. They were killed not by him but by someone who was the ghost of the past, a dead reminder that anything can be corrupted. The stranger fought the monster and won. But only one other survived." She stopped and fell silent.

After a moment Kayle asked. "What can we do to prevent this from happening?"

"Knowing the possibilities can offer you many alternatives. The only way I can see making things different is to act before it happened. Perhaps if you find the stranger before things unfold."

"What does this stranger look like?" Jamas asked.

"I don't remember. I only know he was shrouded in a soft sparkle of blue and silver. The feeling I got was one of sadness and pain. He is coming. And because of his aiding you, he will also die. Not right away. It will be a lingering death. The death of the stranger will mean the end of the long struggle. It will be the beginning of a new battle though. There is never an empty space that is not filled. There must always be balance."

I put away Jamas' journal and wondered at the prediction. So accurate. So like my own dreams. I decided to pick it up again once we got to Egypt.

Somewhere in her notes I knew that she recorded her research on emotional energy and the use of spells. That, coupled with the information I had from Grieta, might give us a powerful weapon in our fight against evil.

The Old Ways

Egypt is an old land. In every stone you can see the story of the beginnings of civilization on our world. Though humanity came from other places, the Nile river was a perfect spot to settle and begin to build. The annual floods were predictable and nourishing. The dry climate preserved the remains of one of the most ancient cultures on our world.

From Cairo we travelled south along the river. There are roads that roughly follow the course of the river on either bank. We chose the western bank as this would lead us through two of the sites I wanted to investigate. We chose the road route simply because we wanted to rent a car so as to be able to react quickly to anything we might find. This way there was no need to charter a boat on the river for just the few of us.

The first stop on our trip would be Deir el-Bahri. One of the temples called Djeser-Djeseru, "Sublime of the Sublimes" in ancient Egyptian, was commissioned by Hatshepsut during her 21-year rule in the early part of the New Kingdom. Hatshepsut's temple was built based some aspects of the older Mentuhotep temple, but on a grander scale.

Illustrations on the walls of Djeser-Djeseru depict Hatshepsut's autobiography. From that I remembered, they detailed her trip to the land of Punt. The river from the Gabarnmung was very similar to what I remembered pictured in the temple. I hoped this would lend us some clue to the possible location of the gate.

The second site was Abu Simbel. Though the entire monument had been moved when the dam that created Lake Nasser was built, I had visited the reconstructed site several times. The overall construction of the drawing at Gabarnmung seemed reminiscent of one of the temple carvings here.

So with only those clues to go on, we drove south through the desert from the capitol city. I felt the continuing effects of the adventure. Both my body and my spirit seemed to be getting weaker as each day passed. The moving meditation of my morning ritual seemed to be less and less effective. My dreams were mostly about death.

Deir el-Bahri stood across the Nile from Luxor and Karnak just a few miles south of the valley of Kings. The temple we were interested in was under the cliff face in the back edge of the complex. This early 18th dynasty structure was considered one of the most incomparable of all ancient Egypt.

The road wound its way along the river. Sometimes we could see the shimmering water and occasionally it was obscured by either dense foliage or because the road wound into the desert. There were numerous towns along the way. We often passed a sign indicating one of the nation's seemingly limitless archeological sites.

It is easy to understand why the country is so intent on its history. The place is steeped in the past. Even from the car we could see monuments standing against the soft blue sky like sentinels standing guard over the Iteru.

I reviewed what I knew of Hatshepsut. Hatshepsut was the chief wife of Thutmose II. Upon his death, she became Pharaoh, ruling from 1473 to 1478 BCE. She was fifth pharaoh of the Eighteenth Dynasty of Egypt, only the second female pharaoh. She ruled as a sort of proxy for Thutmose III, a child of two years old. She is thought of by Egyptologists as one of the most successful rulers of Egypt.

She was a statesman-like ruler that travelled to subject kingdoms and though not as imperialistic as others of the dynasty, she held influence over much of the region outside her own borders.

The famous trip to Punt, which is thought to have been along the eastern African coast, either Somalia or Eritrea, was recorded on the walls of the temple to which we travelled. Though I knew that some of the journey had been along the Nile, at some point the Pharaoh would probably have transferred her ships to the Red Sea for the final leg of the journey.

I was hoping that the mural I remembered would offer some other indication of a potential location. Or at least a few clues as to where to look.

Min had convinced Hector to stay with the team while she returned home to recuperate. He drove the large SUV. I sat next to him studying and thinking about the temple complex we were headed toward. Arianna and Agent Jermyn sat in the middle row seat. Nick and Lucy occupied the rear seat.

The cargo area in the back was full, making viewing through the rearview mirror difficult. Nick had insisted that we maintain clear lines of sight so we moved enough of the gear to the roof rack to allow a minimal field of vision in all directions. Though challenging, Agent Jermyn had secured permits for all of us to retain our side arms.

The drive was relatively long due to the many small towns we passed and the curving nature of the road. Near Sawhaj the highway reduced to one lane in either direction which slowed us even more. Here the occasional farm vehicle would run at very low rates of speed backing up the steady stream of tour busses and other less patient drivers.

For Hector's part, he took it all in stride and never let the traffic bother him. His black rimmed sunglasses and white embroidered shirt made him seem like another one of the tourists. The smile of general congeniality never faded and though he was worried about Min, he never let it show.

My first impression of him had been very confused. Though he could easily be mistaken for someone who might find trouble with the law the norm, he was one of the most well educated and intelligent people I knew.

That was something difficult to imagine considering the company I'd been keeping.

The reality was that each of my friends, which I now considered to be family, was remarkable for their intellect. Though each might have different areas of expertise, they all embodied the very best of what I felt was human nature and ability.

Agent Jermyn and Lucy had withstood the rigor of the fight on the second world. One being active in the final battle and the other acting as a sort of one-person MASH unit for the rest of us.

Nick single handedly faced off the threat of a group of militant cultists in Southeast Asia. He'd proven to be unflappable in the face of corruption and I'd yet to see him loose either his calm or his composure. He seemed to be able to plan his way out of anything.

I continued to feel as though we had the team to complete the mission. Missing Min was a setback but I was hopeful that I could fill her shoes. My one challenge now was that I was the only one in the group that was versed in battling the creatures of corruption using the old traditional ways. Still, I felt sure that we could succeed.

When we finally arrived at the small city, it was much later than I'd anticipated so we decided to cross the Nile and head to our hotel near the airport. We'd decided on the western road so that we might be able to go directly to the temple. This had turned out to be a wasted effort because of the long drive.

Maria and her aunt Doris had several contacts in the archeology community and through these, procured us some time at the site alone. After arriving we invited some of the Egyptologists to join us for a late dinner at the hotel restaurant. Two accepted our invitation.

Dr. Murray was the daughter of an eminent archeologist whose work was highly regarded in academic circles. She had made her home in Egypt after finishing her education and over the last twenty years had become an expert on the women Pharaohs. Though her demeanor was somehow soft spoken and reserved I knew from her reputation that she had a real passion for her work. Her blond short curly hair created a halo of light around her narrow pale face. She had piercing blue eyes that seemed to be too light in color to be natural.

Dr. Ka-nas had been involved in the Egyptian Ministry of Antiquities for the last several decades and was noted as a sort of personality and figurehead of the archeological community in the region. His intellect was sharp however, and I found it difficult to reconcile the man I met with the character he seemed to portray in the documentaries. His slightly heavy frame and naturally easy smile offered a likable and yet somehow stern professor aspect. There was a strange lilt in his accent that seemed to be from another time. When speaking, he would occasionally drop an ending vowel that, coupled with slightly aspirated r's and k's, made it hard to place his origin. Normally I'd have thought him from

Cairo but these aspects were not in any dialect I was aware of.

The mix of academic discussion seemed to inspire all of us including Nick. I'd known he was intelligent but what I discovered during the meal made me excited for him as a member of our team. He'd been studying. From his first exposure to the world of corruption he'd made it his job to investigate the fields of history and archeology. He'd looked into cultural anthropology and social history in order to understand more the opponent as well as the tactics he would need to do battle. Though his research was specific to methodology for combating corruption, he seemed to be able to absorb and understand most of what the experts and academicians at the dinner table offered.

I found myself fully absorbed in the meandering conversation and enjoyed the chance to express a few of my own rather humble ideas about whatever topic presented itself.

Arianna and I both rambled on about the linguistic generalities of the eighteenth dynasty hieroglyphs and possible pronunciation of a few of the more obscure terms. We ended up doing a kind of round-table on word meanings, and potential metaphoric translations that could be used as jokes.

Ka-nas reminded us of an old joke from the Westcar Papyrus that went, "How do you entertain a bored pharaoh? You sail a boatload of young women dressed only in fishing nets down the Nile and tell the pharaoh to go catch a fish."

Through the course of the meal we discussed the site and its many mysteries. Though very well explored, a great deal had yet to be discovered about the Pharaoh Hatshepsut.

Though the topic was well covered, we learned very little new information. In the end, the conversation left us ready to rest in preparation of our private tour of the temple the next day.

As the group dissolved over the course of the evening, conversation became more specific to our task. At last there was only Hector, Arianna, Dr. Murray, Dr. Ka-nas and myself.

Dr. Ka-nas had been a close friend of Doris and Maria. He was well aware of the family vocation and wanted to discuss in private some of the things he'd come to suspect about the dynastic struggles during Hatshepsut's rule.

"You see she ruled jointly with her stepson Thutmose III, he ascended to the throne when he was only 2 years old. She was said to have held the throne for twenty years till the young pharaoh came of age. As the queen and first consort of Thutmose II, she would naturally be in a position to take charge of the country. She was thought of as one of the great rulers of that dynasty. Instead of expanding the empire of Egypt, she built monuments and created trade agreements with many of the surrounding nations."

"The most famous is the trip she took to Punt of course. I understand you have a relic of that trip. Not to worry, I understand it needs to be kept by someone who can be responsible with it. It was described as the round stone that speaks through the mind. Maria says it was broken by the followers of darkness. I wonder, could I see it?"

"Sure." I was hesitant but as Maria trusted him, I felt I could as well. "I'll bring it tomorrow when we view the temple."

"That would be most satisfying. Thank you." His smile warmed at the thought of inspecting the ancient artifact.

"I wonder if you have heard the old tale about the darkness that fills the void?" he asked.

"I am not sure which you mean?" I said genuinely unsure of which version of the story he meant. I should have guessed he would tell me of the old Egyptian tale.

"A darkness, which is evil, fills the void between the worlds. The soul must pass through and be weighed before it can continue to the heavens. But if the heart of the person does not balance the scale then that person is given over to the darkness which fills the void in the Ka, or soul, only then can the person live eternally. The void is between the worlds and it is a place where dreams can become real."

"I have often wondered if the void, the rift, this thing which we now understand to be the mind of the rift, is the thing that the evil one seeks to control," he offered.

"The Master tried once to take control by seeding corruption in the rift but Hector and I managed to drive it out."

"You don't understand my point. You know that evil can exchange mentalities, can possess the mind or the body of another. I think it has been searching for a way to either possess the rift or even to take actual control with its own mentality. To essentially become the rift."

The thought sent a shudder through me. To have the rift's abilities under control of a powerful yet beneficent mind like that of Grieta was one thing. If that power were under the control of evil, there would be no way to stop the spread of corruption. We would be powerless against the most powerful mind in the universe.

Could it be possible? I'd seen for myself that a mind could be transferred into another. A mind could even be combined as it had been with Conner and Keith. Since Grieta was purely a mentality, it seemed almost impossible for a lesser mind to combine and therefore control her. The ancient beings were so far beyond my experience that I had to assume that it could be possible for the Master to overcome Grieta.

Suddenly I realized that we had been so worried about our little battles against the enemy that I had underestimated the situation. The universe was in jeopardy. I wondered if we even had the ability to stop it. I thought we were winning. We had accomplished so much. Now this one revelation seemed to make the whole fight come back into focus. Not only were we not winning, we'd been fighting the wrong battle all along.

The Second Ancient

We walked quietly up the first long ramp toward the main temple. The open courtyard terrace was bounded by the same yellow sandstone which made up most of the temple site. Though relatively close to sea level, the place was dry and depressing for me. I was reminded of the time I'd spent in Egypt as a child digging through the old sites with my parents. These were educational trips we'd gone on between school years. The purpose was my education. I had been expected to learn to read the old writings from a dozen cultures and understand the symbols and their meaning. For a child to have been expected to know so much was, for me, the norm. I'd been to this temple when I was only ten years old and had translated the carvings and frescos with very little error before we finished the summer vacation.

The second ramp took us to the smaller inner terrace. Here, abutted against the rock cliff face was the temple itself. The façade had been built from the same sandstone as the rest of the monument but the temple itself had been carved out of the rock behind. This created a small series of chambers which constituted the center of the funerary complex. Into these we walked.

In the front open section of the temple the ceiling was covered in an exacting pattern of yellow stars on a blue background. Walls were carved and painted in a series of scenes from the life and death of the monarch. Though a few had been purposefully defaced in the later years of the reign of Thutmose III, most were intact enough to infer the original complete picture of the life of the queen.

As I looked at the ceiling of the temple, I realized something I hadn't remembered seeing before. The cobras aligned just below the ceiling seemed similar to another set of carvings I'd seen in India. While I knew the reason for both, I began to wonder how much these old cultures might have interacted.

The RigVedic culture of the Indus valley would have been roughly contemporary and several of the older paintings and carvings from that period were similar to these cobras. Many had hyper-stylized snakes in relief as implements or tools of the various gods of the pre-Vedic cultures.

As my mind wandered, I began to see similarities to other cultures. And in a small section in a lower corner there appeared to be a knot work tri-foil similar to those from early Celtic cultures. One section of it had been worn away over time but it seemed to me that I remembered something like that in an old book from Ireland.

Along one section of the temple wall, the record of the famous trip to Punt was inscribed. Here the story unfolded of the many treasures that the Pharaoh brought back from the newly entreated territory.

Though much had been destroyed, one section that seemed to potentially indicate the geode I now had possession of, told of the powerful artifact that opened the doorway to the land of dreams.

The way it was phrased made me draw my mind back to Ireland. The old legends of a place between worlds where dreams are real and time seems to stop reminded me of the rift. In Celtic legends this place was called Tir Na Nogth, which would appear when the moon was clear as a sort of shadow realm.

The eighteenth dynasty would have been around the time of the Milesian kings of Ireland. Well, two hundred years after the oral traditions say they invaded Ireland to avenge a death. I was aware that this was a proto Celtic culture but that the bronze age was well underway and trade had been established with Wales and other areas of Britain.

As my mind digressed into a review of ancient history, I remembered that each of these cultures also had lengthy legends about the battle between good and evil. Also each of the Drakson family seemed to find some affinity for one or more of the old cultures.

Zach had been very interested in Greek and Etruscan history. Jamas was definitely influenced by Asian traditions, Kayle seemed to have immersed himself with Northern European and old Celtic lore. Stevanie's spells were built around Latin and Egyptian cores. Thomas was well versed in both Greek and Persian cultures. Finally, Maria had somehow managed to study such a wide variety of historical material as to be well founded in everything she'd been exposed to.

This indicated to me that each culture had some ties to the others and that, as we learned about the Manandan Indians, these cultures regularly interacted. The most ancient secret society had been developed not around building world power. It had been formed to protect humanity from the Master, and from the corruption which we now knew had its origins in humanity.

Dr. Ka-nas brought me back to the present with the question I knew he was bound to ask.

"Can I see the geode?"

"Sure," I replied hesitantly. "It's right here."

I reached into my backpack and withdrew a leather wrapped bundle of about eight inches in diameter. Slowly I unwrapped the parcel revealing the sandy stone shell with whitish crystals in the interior.

The gasp of joy from both him and Dr. Murray made me smile. I felt that way every time I looked at it too. Though in many ways it was nothing other than an ordinary split geode, a feeling of joy or optimism seemed to rise in me every time I looked into the clear prisms that formed the interior of the rock.

Almost without thinking, I mentally repeated the chant activating the lens and therefore opening the gateway to Grieta, the rift.

A deep and abiding happiness filled me as I felt her presence. I'd been told that when someone is in love they feel this sense of desire and purpose for the person of their affection. I had begun to wonder if I was capable of love. Not the romantic form but a deep and true love.

Each time I heard the soft yet powerful voice of Grieta in my mind, I knew that I could indeed love. Even if the reason for it was simply that my mind was unprepared to fathom the true nature of Grieta. I felt joy.

"Hello," I said.

"Hello," she said back. I felt a definite level of comfort in the voice. She and I had become friends over the last two years and each time we conversed I felt the happiness of renewed contact.

"You know everyone here with the exception of Dr. Murray and Dr. Ka-nas," I introduced them. "Doctors, this is the Rift which I have come to call Grieta."

"I am very pleased to meet you," Dr. Murray said in a slight Scottish accent.

"Me as well," Dr. Ka-nas bowed slightly to indicate respect.

"Chris has offered us a chance to know his work and to aid him. I had heard the legends of the stone but never truly believed them until now. I am your humble servant," he concluded and bowed again, this time more deeply.

"No," said Grieta. "You need not serve or be served. We are partners in our fight against the evil we face. We face it together and though I can only act in very small ways, I will help you, each of you, as best I can."

"Thank you," I said. I could feel a slight distancing of her mind from us and wondered if she was wary of either of our new companions. The problem with these thoughts when conversing with Grieta was obvious and something I had known for some time. My thoughts were transmitted to everyone in the room. I decided to make it a formal question.

"Is there something wrong?" I asked.

"The one you call Dr. Ka-nas, has used the gate you possess before. In the old days he was its keeper."

"Really," I looked over at the doctorand mentally confronted him. "How long ago?"

"Four centuries more or less. But the truth is I am older than that even." As he explained, his gaze lowered to the floor. "I am one of the four. It was I who gave away the secret of corruption to the Master. I have taken the body of the man you see here in the earliest part of the time you call the eighteenth dynasty. I tried to help my friend Be Chot Shi Ti defend humanity from our companion." Things stood still for a moment. We seemed unable to move or comment on the revelation that we were in the presence of both the rift and one of the four ancients. I asked the obvious question.

"What happened to Begotsidi? What happened to him?"

"Begotsidi, you called him? Destroyed by the evil Da Ra Cha Ti, the one that became known as the Master. When humans were brought back to their old world, to repopulate and rebuild, Da Ra Cha Ti found my friend and bound him into the roots of a tree. The tree was at the base of a mountain of fire. When the volcano erupted, Be Chot Shi Ti was destroyed. Once bound to a physical form, we must obey the laws of the form, so the tree burned and my friend died."

"I'm sorry." My condolences rang a little empty. "How have you survived then? Humans cannot live four thousand years."

"But you can," the ancient advised. "If free of disease, a human body is easy to repair. Simple mechanics of cell structure and regeneration. The mentality in the body can be eternal if given the proper care. Oh, men are fragile in many ways. But also resilient. The mind can do so much given the focus and power to achieve."

"My mentality is not bound to this world. Like the rift, I can draw energy from the universe. It is a simple thing to use it to maintain the body I now inhabit."

"There was a simple side effect, however. Without access to the gateway device, the geode, I was trapped on this world. Now I can be free to continue my travels and explore eternity."

"I'm sorry," I told him. "I'm charged with protecting the gate. I can't let you have it. As much as I believe you are a good person, I can't risk it falling into the hands of one of the minions of corruption. I hope you understand."

"You seem to be holding all the cards. I have waited these many centuries. I can wait some time more. I urge you to let me have the one once you have completed your task. Also should you fail, let me know where the gate is kept so that I might retrieve it and make my way on my own."

"With your knowledge and experience, we could work together to put an end to this," I said hopefully. "Da Ra Cha Ti wouldn't stand a chance against us if we banded together." I felt easier calling him Da Ra Cha Ti instead of the Master. It always seemed a little overbearing a title and he wasn't my master anyway.

It's said, knowing a person's name give you some power over them. With everything I'd learned in the last few years I was prepared to believe that. In a way, the power you gain over them is a sort of familiarity, a humanization of the intangible. The thing we fought against wasn't just some evil entity that couldn't be fathomed, it had a name and therefore it was closer to our level than I'd ever thought it could be.

Maybe it was old, ancient even, but it was still a thing that had an identity. It's identity and its will to survive and control the universe made it a person in a way. I felt better about our chances than I had in quite a while.

I also felt content and happy due to the continuing contact with Grieta. If I couldn't persuade Dr. Ka-nas to join our cause, then perhaps she could.

Before the thought was fully realized, I knew the answer. Grieta wouldn't interfere with this person's freedom of choice. She had said as much to me and therefore to all of us. She felt it was up to each of us to determine our own path. That was why she had helped humanity confront Da Ra Cha Ti. If we lost our ability to choose for ourselves, we would be lost.

Maybe it was only academic anyway. The argument that anyone truly had freedom of choice seemed lost on me. I'd been drawn into the war against evil without having been consulted or given the chance to say no. Oh, I guess I could have left and let Maria Drakson and others fight on without me. That wasn't the kind of person I was. The old comic book hero in me was still trying to save the day. So it is true to say I had some choice, but there really wasn't any choice other than the one I made.

"I agree that you should have access to the geode once we finish. And I also agree that if we fail, you may claim it. I feel like our chances would have been better if you were to help us though," I said.

Dr. Murray entered the conversation at that point. "What is this you are talking about? Corruption? Evil? Ancient beings? Grieta and the gateways?"

"I suppose you deserve an explanation as much as anyone. Now that you have heard." I said.

"Let me?" Grieta offered. "I can transfer the memories to her quickly so that you need not tell the entire story. One moment and she will understand all. I've done this before and the effects might be a little surprising at first. Once the memories are transferred though, you will understand all that we face."

I had not thought of the possibility of transferring a memory. Transferring an entire mentality was possible, why would a memory be so difficult? I was beginning to understand that what consciousness really was, was a specific ordered element of memories held together by intelligent organization. At the center of these memories was what some might call the soul.

I felt a sort of mental tickling. I guess that would be the best way to describe it. Then a rush of memories pushed into my consciousness starting at the Drakson house two years ago and culminating with our current adventure. Every moment from then till now, played quickly through my mind. It felt like I was reliving the time on fast forward. Each emotion and each thought felt intensified by the rapid and unrelenting tide of the transfer. I felt loss, joy, fear, love, run in and through me. Each feeling ran to the next and tears of joy mingled to become tears of pain.

Through all of it I did as I always have done. My mind distanced itself from the feelings, unable to understand my own reaction I delved into the mechanical of the experience and analyzed the process. It was another wall to protect me from my own emotional disaster. So I retreated and hid in my scientific and unfeeling fortress against the world.

What struck me as odd was that I reviewed the memories from the point of view I would have taken when I use my ability to see into the past. In essence, I observe someone else's memories. I knew it was because Dr. Murray would be reviewing my memories from the point of view of an observer. I was seeing my memories from another person's point of view. It offered me a rare and somehow disturbing contradiction to my own original experience. In a way it had the effect of intensifying the emotional quality of the memories. Dr.

Murray was more in tune with her own emotions and therefore felt similar yet different as the emotions and memories were made available to her.

Once the transfer was complete, an odd sensation of lightness and freedom overcome me. The heavy, deep emotions faded to the background. It was as though a great weight had been taken from my shoulders. The tingle of the transfer faded and was replaced by the same overwhelming joy that I always feel when in contact with Grieta.

“Oh my,” said Dr. Murray. “Oh my.” As she began to weep, she put her hands over her face and dropped to her knees.

“I’m sorry,” Grieta apologized. “The memories are strong and somewhat painful. I had not expected this response.”

“I’m ok,” Murray replied. “Just, how can anyone go through all that and not feel like crying.”

Dark Creature

Contact had been dropped for about an hour. We stayed in the back section of the temple waiting for Dr. Murray to fully recover from the emotional ordeal. She was somewhat shaken by the effect. Being honest, I had been shaken by it too.

Places have memories just as people do. When strong emotional situations occur, powerful forces of energy are released into the surrounding environment. They linger for quite some time. With proper training I'd learned to interpret these residual memories.

Something that I had come to understand recently was that magic is powered by emotion. Memories are conduits of emotion. So if a person were to invoke a specific memory, the resulting emotional response to that memory might be used to energize a spell.

I wanted to get back to Jamas's diary to see what she had discovered on the subject. So far my conjecture had been somewhat fruitless as I hadn't had an opportunity to test any theories.

A sound from the opening in the temple startled us. It seemed to be a cross between a low rumble and a hiss. There followed a shuffling as though someone were dragging themselves along the stone floor of the temple.

When we looked back to the opening through which we had entered, we could see very little as the light shown in brightly, making it impossible to see anything against its glare. Still some weird movement at the bottom drew our attention and as our gaze settled on the shuffling figure, it became apparent the noise had been made by something other than man.

As it cleared the door frame, its shape came into focus. The long winding body on four short stilts of legs was obviously a crocodile. There was some disturbing deformity of the spine and head that included several rows of broken, spike-like projections that seemed both familiar and terrifying. In the gloom, a green and silver glitter could be seen shining in the small eyes. Elongated and curved claws now jutted several inches from the humanlike hands and feet. At the end of the tail several of the ridges jutted upward like the spikes on a stegosaurus.

When we had encountered the possessed corpses of Mathias Drakson, similar projections covered his body. It was a sign of corruption that gave no room for doubt.

The crocodile's head swayed left then right as though searching for something. Then in such a rapid motion as to scare us to our wits end, it raised itself slightly on its legs and dashed toward Dr. Murray. In less than a second it had gripped her left leg just above the knee.

Nick raised a pistol which he'd drawn from its hip holster and fired several shots directly into the thing's head. This seemed to startle it some as it released Dr. Murray and turned toward him. In another rapid motion it charged him.

By this time, I had my focus restored and formed the keywords to activate a barrier spell around Nick. The lettering which ran down the left sleeve of my shirt vanished as the spell took shape. The creature slowed, then stopped short and turned away from its prey as though it could no longer stand the sight of the intended victim.

Lucy moved over to the injured archeologist to see if she could offer her aid.

As it tried to recover, Hector pointed his large silver piston at it and fired a single shot.

The creature ran toward the exit at the new pain we'd caused. As it passed, it slowed and took another snipping bite at Dr. Murray, leaving a long gash in her left arm as well.

Lucy was forced to recoil backward into the sunlight as the creature continued to slowly press forward. I refused to let her be injured and ran toward the thing. Though it was passing the threshold, its tail was still in the shadow of the inner temple. A combat spell I'd created to blast at the internal organs of a corrupted creature had been primed and leapt off the seam of my pant leg.

The entire rear portion of the crocodile seemed to explode in a shower of corruption. Though there was no other physical sign of its effect, the spell expelled corruption in a violent metaphysical explosion.

The crocodile simply slumped to the floor and ceased moving. It had been dead before I activated the spell. Without the influence of corruption to animate the thing, it reverted to an inanimate death.

Lucy had tripped on the base of one of the broken columns in the courtyard. Though slightly bruised, she was otherwise unharmed. I escorted her back inside to see what could be done about Dr. Murray.

The bites in the leg and arm were both deep and bled profusely. Lucy had already opened her medical bag and withdrawn several heavy gauze pads to use as pressure bandages. These she retrieved from the floor where she'd dropped them and began the process of packing the jagged bites to stem the loss of blood.

As she worked on the arm, she had me aid her by placing pressure on the wounds of the leg. Once that was done, we switched places and she began to work on the more frightful yet less lethal injury.

Again she packed gauze into the wound and wrapped it in a heavy bandage. A pool of blood had formed around the doctor and our knees had become soaked in the sticky warm fluid.

As Lucy finished the second bandage, Dr. Murray let out a loud sigh and stopped breathing. Lucy checked for a pulse and found none.

Lucy immediately began CPR. I'd been coached in the technique so I assisted as we ran through the two-person drill. Lucy compressed then stopped for me to give the two breaths required. After checking for a pulse again she nodded and we resumed.

Dr. Ka-nas had called for medical rescue. We could hear the wail of the ambulance speeding toward us in the distance. Still, Lucy and I continued to work on reviving our new friend.

It felt like an eternity waiting for help. How long could we bear the slowly increasing sound of aid as we feverishly bent over Dr. Murray? The long series of compressions followed by two short breaths repeated over and over and... Lucy checked the pulse again. A sadness came over her face but she nodded for us to continue.

Finally, I felt a hand on my shoulder and looked up to see the medic who shifted into position, taking my place. Another technician moved in across from Lucy and relieved her of her onerous duty. A third medic set up a portable defibrillator which was on a gurney they'd hauled up the entire length of the temple ramp.

I stood back and watched in a daze as they continued to try to bring the doctor back. Each time they checked, there was no sign of life. After two rounds of defibrillation, they called the time and laid a white sheet from the gurney over her face.

The team was downcast. We'd all seen a lot of death in our time together but it still had a deeply emotional effect on each of us. Even the rather stoic personality of Nick had creased with tears as they rolled the body down the steps and into the waiting ambulance.

After some small investigation, the authorities concluded that the crocodile attack was simply a rare occurrence and that we had been lucky to be armed otherwise we'd be in worse shape. The misshapen form of the crocodile was readied for removal by whatever authorities do that sort of thing while Nick and Hector showed their permits for carrying firearms.

After several hours we were allowed to return to our hotel with instructions to await an official conclusion which would probably be vetted and signed on the following day.

By then the evening had crept up and we were all famished and exhausted. I retired to my room and ordered a small plate from room service.

Where had the crocodile come from? If possessed, it needed a gateway to allow the possessing mentality through. If on the other hand it were simply controlled by corruption, the creature could have been created by an agent of corruption. It seemed possible that something dogged our steps.

For us to have encountered one creature in Australia and then another in Egypt seemed too much of a coincidence. The more I thought about it, the more I knew that we might have a potentially more pressing problem. Maybe we were being spied upon and followed by our enemy.

I couldn't help but think that Dr. Murray's death could have been avoided if I'd known we were under the watchful eye of evil. My mind kept wandering back to the pool of blood into which I knelt, trying desperately to keep her alive. I had failed miserably on that account. I was beginning to wonder if I had the chops to do this job. My confidence seemed to be slipping.

I needed to get my head into the game again. It was the only way to keep from thinking about the events of the day. Jamas' journal lay as I had left it on the left hand nightstand. Now was a good time to evade my mental anguish by submerging myself into research.

I opened the journal to the napkin marking the place I'd left off.

Jamas seemed interested in detailing a variety of techniques for creating spells that could be used in more practical ways than simply fighting corruption.

Most magic is not like people think. In general, it effects only creatures which have come into direct contact with corruption. That is to say magic effects the corruption in these creatures. This is due to the metaphysical nature of corruption. Simply put, magic has no effect on the real tangible world, or at least that was the original theory.

Some time ago Maria had been working on a way of using magic to create real effects. And during our time in the second world, magic was as real as science is in our world. Each world has a unique set of rules. The reason magic had been so powerful in the second world was that the fabric of the world was composed of energy that could be used to power a spell.

If a person could find a method to power a spell in our world, then real world effects could be possible. Jamas had begun studying the use of emotion to do just that. I had known that Maria and Jamas both had been trained by their mother separately, and therefore used magic slightly differently than their siblings.

Further reading showed that Jamas had tried using martial arts as a way of expressing emotion and capturing the energy for use. There are several forms of Chinese soft style arts that are founded on the idea that each action had a relevant emotion required to power it.

A punch might require a moment of anger or a certain kick might be powered by a fluid expression of joy. It seemed possible that similar movements could be incorporated into the semantics of the spell casting and offer a foundation upon which a caster might create very powerful spells.

Jamas warned that using too much emotion too quickly might cause permanent harm to the spell caster. Also there seemed to be a cumulative effect. The more you cast spells using this technique the more a slave of your own emotions you are likely to become. Slowly over time you could lose the ability to control emotions outside of the spell casting environment. As with everything else I'd learned since meeting the Draksons, there seemed to be dangers.

In the end I felt like it was worth pursuing anyway as I was not long for the world. My impending death seemed to have freed me to continue the more dangerous aspect of my studies without fear. So I'd die from corruption getting me or from a spell gone horribly wrong. I'd be dead either way.

As I continued reading, I realized that Jamas had encountered evil which she at first took to be part and parcel of the war against corruption but which she later determined to be of another nature all together. I'll relate the story in the next few chapters so that you can understand and I think it is salient to the continuing relevance of our team if we manage to thwart Da Ra Cha Ti.

I hadn't really thought too much about the idea that there might be evil other than that which was associated with corruption. It stood to reason though, after having heard about the ancients and human history that evil must have existed before they became involved in the affairs of people.

I began to suspect that evil as a concept had been around from the very beginning of consciousness and would be something that needed guarding against as long as people had the imagination to control and place themselves above others.

There must also be other beings in the universe that would fit into the mold of evil. Maybe they would use other tools to control and destroy. Maybe other methods would be employed in the fight against those particular versions of evil. There would be the need to continue to do just that.

I even imagined that once free of the clutches of Da Ra Cha Ti, many of his minions might seek to fill the vacuum.

All of this assumed we could defeat this one adversary. Afterword, those that survive would be free to debate the future course of actions needed for the protection of the world.

The Darkness of the Dead

She stood in a dark corner of the overcrowded room. Though the flashing lights seemed to find every spot in the loud room she somehow remained in the shadows. Her dark skin and angular features indicated she might be a descendant of a Northeastern Native American tribe but no one in the room would have known.

The disco was filled with a conglomeration of Asians mixed with the few others. Most were typically olive skinned with almond shaped eyes. A few were Caucasian. They all seemed embroiled in the music save for two.

The woman in the dark corner and a man standing near the bar.

The man seemed Asian though his skin was somewhat pale. His hair was bleached and almost pure white. If it were not for the smooth youthful complexion, he might have been mistaken for an old man.

He leaned against a black painted pillar. His gaze swept the room as though he were looking for someone. Occasionally he'd smile a predatory smile then continue to observe the crowd. From a distance, the woman in the corner could tell he was evil.

His smile told of a lust for death. The mocking brow, and contemptuous sneer gave little room for doubt. This was the man she'd been looking for. She wondered if he knew he was being hunted.

Jamas was taking a risk. Here in a foreign country, she had heard rumors of a killer. After seeing the methods he employed, she knew he was evil. She felt compelled to do something to protect those that could not protect themselves. In this case, she decided that included the police who had been entrusted to safeguard life.

Three police officers had died and another was in critical condition. A dozen people were known to have been victims of the killer. The police still had no leads other that the general m.o. of the culprit.

Jamas had reviewed the information and decided on a plan of action. That plan led her to the disco where she sat in silence waiting for signs of corruption. An hour earlier she'd taken a very small dose of the glittery powder that would allow her to detect the presence of evil.

There he was. Not thirty feet from her. He stood at the end of the bar snapping his fingers occasionally, not quite in time with the music.

His gaze landed on a young Japanese woman sitting at the other end of the bar alone.

It was obvious she'd drank too much as her head nodded from side to side in a loose and unnatural way. She seemed unable to focus on anything other than the drink she held in her shaking hand. As she stood to leave, she stumbled into another patron who admonished her for her public intoxication.

The pale man straightened as he saw her stumble toward the door. He fastened the lower of the two buttons on his expensive tailored suit. In a natural and easy motion, he intercepted the woman. Slipping an arm under hers, he escorted her toward the door, all the while whispering in her ear.

Jamas stood and followed as they exited through the large glass double door.

The parking garage on the other side of the door stood several stories high. Though well lit, the florescent lights created large pools of dark shadow along the edges of the open space. Each floor contained more than forty cars. Almost every space was taken.

By the time Jamas reached the door, the man and his prey had crossed to an expensive sports car at the far end of the upward sloping ramp.

The man pushed the woman roughly into the passenger seat then began to cross to the driver's side when Jamas caught up to them.

“You can’t have her!” she shouted in fluent Japanese. Though she was only a few yards away, the force of her conviction added power to her demand.

“You can’t stop me,” he replied in English. “She is not yours to protect, witch!” The contempt in his voice was evident.

“I won’t let you take her,” Jamas interjected. “I will protect her.”

“I suspect this is going to get ugly,” came the response. “You are half dazed on the dust. Do you really think you have a chance against my power?” he asked.

With that, he stretched forth his hand and pressed his will against that of his adversary.

Jamas said a few words and struck a pose as though she were about to engage in a kung fu fight movie scene. A series of Chinese characters from the sleeve of her right arm disappeared as she finished speaking the words. This engaged her in the battle against the man.

A battle of wills is particularly boring for those that might be viewing the effects. The opponents stand silent and unmoving. It is a staring contest of the mind. Each presses the power of will, its force, against the other. Slowly, meticulously the being with the stronger will begins to press back against the weaker. If one combatant is a great deal stronger than the other, he or she may force the other to obey their bidding. When equally matched, the results are less spectacular.

This battle was very closely matched. In general, the man had more powerful will, but Jamas had the power of purpose on her side, lending strength. Her conviction of righteousness, gave the edge she needed to equal her enemy.

After what seemed like hours but was mere seconds, each knew that a battle of wills would not result in an easy outcome. The man broke it off and took the old route of physical attack.

He closed the gap between the two and leaned into a punch that would have resulted in a contusion of the heart had it connected. Instead, Jamas stepped to the side easily and blocked with her forearm, her hands open and rigid in a knife like posture. Her legs were wide and her feet perfectly parallel. The angle of her arms was perfectly aligned, fingertips of the left to the elbow of the right.

For less than a heartbeat she froze, waiting for the monster to move. She preferred a defensive posture till she understood his attacking method. The next attack told her all she needed to know.

He spun lightly on his heal and swung a rather unbalanced kick to her midsection.

She slipped back just enough to avoid the clumsy attempt and shifted her arms to the opposite pose. Once the leg swung around, she stepped in behind it and pushed the palm of her left hand into the lower back of the man. The man stumbled backward, off balance.

Jamas followed quickly and slipped a low kick at his now extended leg. Without setting it back down she followed with a kick to his face. Then she leaned into him and drove her right elbow across into his now exposed throat.

He slipped backward in desperation, barely avoiding the attack. Now leaning against the car, he gripped the door handle and lifted both legs and in a rolling motion, flipped back over the car. The effect was to place the car between him and Jamas.

It was obvious now that Jamas was more skilled at hand fighting and this seemed to frighten the man. He looked this way and that seemingly searching for a way to escape. His enhanced physical abilities should have made Jamas an easy target. How could a simple human defeat him?

The answer was simple. Jamas was not a normal human. In fact, she'd studied all her life to fight evil such as this man possessed. He'd called her a witch. Though not technically true, it served as a reminder that she had discipline enough to battle even the likes of him and his fellows.

Fear raged into his eyes as he realized he could not win. Since he'd been changed he had not known fear. His maker had said that darkness was his ally, secrecy his only real weapon. Now both eluded him. He ran.

Jamas was now torn between the need to stop him and the need to help the woman he'd tried to abduct. If the pattern were as she imagined, his evil would already be spreading into her. She decided then to make sure of the safety of the woman before pursuing the man.

She sat in the front seat slumped forward. Jamas checked her pulse and realized that she was still alive but the unsteady and inconsistent beat told her that he'd already begun to infect her.

There are literally dozens of undead creatures in the world. Vampires, ghosts, wraiths, and may more have been created by the forces of evil. Some are tools of the Master, others are simply creatures of evil fighting to survive and feed in a world of the living. There are a few that believe they can regain their humanity by devouring the life force or even the flesh of those that are without corruption. Such is a wight.

The mentality of the creature is bonded to a recently deceased body. If it feeds on the flesh of the living quickly it can stop the body from rotting away. The legends say that if it consumes enough uncorrupted flesh, the wight can regain its humanity.

When a person is exposed to the spirit of the wight, it begins to decay. Slowly the body will die and the person will be faced with the choice: to seek a new body and become a wight or fade into oblivion. Most good minds realize the truth and chose not to embrace the evil that consumes them. A few, chose the chance at life.

The fact that the woman was drunk, and unable to form an intelligible thought, meant she would probably not understand the choice. She would probably decide to live. Or, really she would decide not to die. She could then become a terror, feeding on humanity from the shadows.

Jamas had only one spell that might work for this situation. Imprinted on the center seam of her blouse along the line of buttons at the front, was a healing spell. She'd need to adjust it slightly to account for the touch of darkness from the creature.

She would need a little room to perform the needed ritual.

Pulling the woman from the car, she placed her in an open area behind it. This was in the line of traffic but it couldn't be helped. There was no other place where she'd have enough room to make the proper mechanics.

In a low stance she moved in slow, precise, intent movements designed to draw out the corrupting influence. The dance of energy seemed almost like the

Yang style of Tai Chi. When she lowered into a deep bow stance, her crane's head hand touched just to the left of the heart of the woman. As she rose, a thin line of black and grey smoke rose from the spot and quickly dissipated into nothing.

The woman seemed to breathe easier once the smoke was gone. Color returned to her face and she sighed a soft sigh before pursing her lips and falling into a deep sleep.

The enemy had escaped. Jamas was prepared to wait for him to try again. She knew that he'd move on though. Now that he was discovered, he'd find a new place to seek his salvation. What the undead do not understand is that nothing can give them back their humanity. Once tainted they are forever in the grasp of evil. You can never return from death. The will to live is strong even in the dead. The need to love and hope and touch is a powerful incentive to do whatever it takes to regain what was lost. The illusion of living is all that is attainable. Part of the natural cycle of life is that we must all die. In death we consummate our lives. In life we must accept that death is the final outcome. Jamas wrote in her journal that we can accept death knowing that in life we have done what we could to be the best person we needed to be. What other reason to live than to sacrifice for those we love?

The Desolate Places of the Earth

I woke with a shudder. Breathing deeply the dry cool desert air, I felt disoriented and cold. The rough texture of sand below me made me think I was still sleeping and that this was a dream. I closed my eyes again and tried to wake myself up. That didn't work. I was already awake.

The last thing I remember was laying down to sleep in the hotel bed after having read a long section of Jamas' journal. So the question was, how had I gotten here?

I searched my memory and came up short. I hadn't any memory since the onset of my dreams. Dreams of being spirited away by the hands of heaven.

I stood and looked around. There was nothing on the ground to reveal my location. It was dark still. Thousands of stars twinkled brightly in the sky. I looked around the horizon to see if there were any clues to my whereabouts. To one direction I could see the pale glow of light pollution creating a thin line of silhouette on the horizon.

Looking up at the stars, I found the pole star and checked the position of the other stars around and determined that I was probably at a close latitude to Luxor. If the first assumption was correct, the general position of the stars seemed to indicate a time of approximately 2:00 AM.

The light from the city seemed to be to the east. Its intensity made me think I was perhaps twenty miles from Luxor. This would have put me on the west side of the river and not far from the temple we'd visited earlier.

I tried to get my bearings. Again I made some assumptions and then made the decision to begin walking in a north easterly direction. My hope was that I'd intersect the M75 in a few miles – hopefully not more than four.

At average foot speed in the desert I might make it by 3:15 AM. Though a dozen possibilities ran through my head, I decided not to answer the question of how I'd gotten where I was till I managed to get out of danger.

There is a general feeling that one might be safe so close to a city. This is not really the case. While much of the world has been tamed my human activity, there are great tracks of land that are still as wild as when man first discovered fire. People had been living in the Nile valley for as long as human memory could record and yet there was a wildness to the area surrounding the cities that could never be penetrated by man. Here in the desert, a man could die from exposure to the sun, or from the elements that sapped a person of the will to continue.

I, a dying man, had a desire to live. I began my walk as though I would a walk in a park in the middle of a city. I felt that I would simply come to the end of the walk and take a nice hot shower and feel refreshed, ready to continue my purpose. Ready to fight the good fight. I felt ready to do anything I needed to, to finish the battle I'd started two years before.

Maybe that sounds somewhat narcissistic. I'd never been wanting for confidence. Most of my life I'd felt so far removed from the general population that I'd scarcely given a thought to failing. So I walked.

Walking in the desert was slower than I'd hoped. I felt as though I was making less than three miles in an hour and had yet to come upon the M75 in the first hour. But I felt I needed to keep going. If there was one thing kept me from panicking, it was a cool night. In a few hours, the sun would rise and I'd have to contend with the heat as well as the feeling of loneliness.

The truth was that I had been used to being lonely. That was before I'd met the Draksons. Since then I had come to cherish the familial connection I'd earned with Maria and the others.

I guess it's easy to say so now. That I felt an affinity for these few people that touched my heart. The truth was that just a few years before I'd been unable to connect in anyway with anyone.

My walk in the desert was simply another test in which I knew the answer. I had to get back to those that mattered the most to me. I had to get back to my family.

I've suggested before that I felt a familial connection to Hector, Min, Maria, Arianna, Nick, Conner, Lucy, and the others. There is an underlying truth to the statement. I would have done anything to make sure that each of them was free of the evil which we all faced.

I continued to think of them as I trudged through the sands of the desert. Occasionally I'd look into the sky and gauge my progress. I'd nod and smile knowing that I'd make it back to the team before they even knew I had been gone.

My foot landed upon something solid and unyielding. I looked around for some indication of what it might be. A dark tower of rock seemed to obscure the light from the distant city. I could see the halo of light that marked my goal around the tall regular blackness. Perhaps I'd managed to come to one of the many archeological sites that bounded the Nile. It seemed to me to be a sign of good omen. I must be getting close.

If it was in fact a site that had been uncovered then at some point the following day, there would be visitors. Perhaps an academic or simply tourists, maybe a tour guide. I felt the pressure of finding civilization fade from my thoughts and I began to wonder where I might be.

I was dressed in my pajamas which were light and thin cotton. My feet had been worn smooth from the sand I'd trudged through for the last few hours. How many hours?

I looked into the sky to check the time. Nearly four in the morning. A faint light was showing above the horizon to the east indicating a coming dawn. If my memory served, dawn would be around five thirty. I'd have decent light to see in much less time.

I decided to wait here and figure out exactly where I was. If this were a recorded site, I'd be able to recognize the features and know for sure. Even if I didn't know the site, I would at least be able to continue to wait in a shady place till the sun went down and I could continue on. Without water, my chances of survival depended on conservation.

While I waited, I contemplated how I'd gotten here. I had been sleeping. I didn't wake up at any point and I don't remember having been disturbed at all. My mind seemed unable to fathom the problem.

Light slowly gave me a clearer picture of my surroundings. I'd never seen this location before and I didn't recognize any features save two large monoliths. These flanked a rather ordinary looking building front. They bore no decoration and seemed made of single long pillars of the red quartz stone that comprise many of the monuments in the general area. They'd probably been imported from a distant quarry.

I tried to remember all the varied sites in the general area. None that came to my mind were consistent with the features of the buildings here. I didn't remember any obelisks without hieroglyphics from the eighteenth dynasty. To be truthful, I was not the expert on Egyptian archeology. So I was without any new information to help in my attempt to get back to the hotel and my friends.

As the morning grew more light, I wandered the small escarpment of stone which made up the face of the temple building. Like many other sites from its time, it had been carved into the face of the rock behind. The overall effect was very similar to Hatshepsut's temple where we'd spent the day before. The main difference was the absence of writing or decoration on any of the surfaces.

I'd wondered if the sand may have worn away any impressions that would have been carved long ago. The general sharpness of the stone in appearance made me think that there never had been any adornment to this place.

I entered through the main opening and continued down a passage that went for some thirty feet before it opened to a large chamber some fifty feet to a side. Along the opposite wall was another passage that led deeper into the rock face. Each wall had several nooks where statues of gods would have stood in any other temple. There were no such decorations here.

Perhaps this site had been unfinished, somehow forgotten in time. It would explain the lack of features and the overall feeling of incompleteness that followed as I looked through the remaining chambers at the back. Again, nothing more than the walls and general structure.

A feeling of disappointment started to overtake me. The sun was now up and warming the sands outside. If this was a site that people visited there would be a chance of rescue soon. If not, I'd need to stay here for the day before continuing my trek across the desert tonight after sundown.

The feeling I'd been fighting seemed to be getting more and more palpable. It seemed to include fear now. Was I feeling fear that I'd die alone here in the temple that no one knew? Or was there something more? The tightness in my chest intensified. I felt terrified.

I knew this feeling well. The fear was no natural fear. It came from a creature invested in corruption. I felt its gaze on my back and turned to face the thing that gave me such agonizing terror.

They say that in knowing something you remove its ability to cause you fear. I can say from my own experience the saying is not as true as I wish it were.

There in the shadow of one of the niches stood a creature of darkness. I could sense corruption feeding through it. Usually I needed to concentrate to use the ability to sense corruption. This was a check against the very effect I now tried in vain to fight.

Corruption created a halo of blinding darkness and sparkling energy to radiate from the creature. I could not make out any details due to the intense onslaught of the radiated glamour. The only thing I could tell was, this was a living being that stood like a human. Perhaps it was a person who had given their life over to the darkness.

I chanted a small spell to focus my energy and diminish the effect that blinded me. My pajamas did not have any spell woven into them, though, so I was forced to add a power channeling component to the spell. This added several seconds during which I was vulnerable to attack. I curled into a ball and fell to the floor as I finished pouring energy into the spell.

I felt the force of the blow which landed on the small of my back. It felt as though I'd been hit by a hammer. The second blow landed near the base of my neck causing stars and nearly breaking my focus.

As I felt the effect of my spell building, I uncurled and rolled away from the attacks. I swung to my feet in a windmill like motion I'd learned in one of the many martial arts classes I'd taken as a child. As I turned to face my enemy, I heard the running footsteps that signaled an approach.

I looked at a dark skinned man in his middle years. Black hair and sparkling eyes gave him an eastern aspect. Though fully shaved, his face reminded me of the desert. He wore the clothing of a nomad. Long and slightly dirty, his robes left only his hands and face exposed.

I blocked the punch he threw at my face easily. A quick side step gave me an opening to strike at his exposed ribs. I knifed my fingers quickly at the lower end, hoping to break the smaller ribs that don't connect to the sternum. My attack was too low and I only succeeded in forcing the air from his lungs.

He doubled over as he expelled a heavy breath. This gave me the chance to strike anywhere along the back I wanted. Just below the base of the neck there is a little notch that signifies the joint of the main spinal column with the lighter vertebrae of the neck. It is a landmark for the trained martial artists. Just above this junction, a well-placed blow can cause trauma to the spin which results in temporary paralysis.

I swung my leg in a large arc. My kick landed just above the bottom of the cervical curve.

A loud sign issued from the man and he fell in a heap on the stone floor at my feet. I could see that his eyes rolled back and forth but he seemed astonished that he could not command his own body to move. A raspy voice asked me what I had done.

"Don't worry," I said. "I haven't killed you. Before I do, I need a little information. Maybe if I get what I want, I'll let you live."

"I cannot tell you what I do not know. I know nothing!" he spat back at me.

"You know why I was separated from my friends and that you were here to attack me," I said dryly. "Maybe there are other things you can tell me. For instance, where are we?"

"We are in the desert. I followed as I was instructed. I was told to kill you if I found you alone and I did find you alone here in the temple. I attacked. What more is there?" he replied.

"How did you get me here?" My query seemed reasonable.

"I didn't bring you here. I followed." Again he seemed to be mocking me.

"Ok. Do you know how I got here?" I asked trying to find a chink in his metal.

"You walked." The smile on his face was beginning to bother me.

"I meant how did I get in the desert, away from the city?" My frustration was beginning to show and the man lying on the floor knew it.

"Yes." He knew he was in control of the conversation even though he couldn't control his own body. I needed to change the status.

"All right then. That's something," I smiled. I can let you go, or I can simply let you die," I lied. "The choice is up to you."

"Why would you? You hate everything that I stand for. Everything that I am. Why let me go?" he asked.

"Maybe that's what good people do," I said knowing I would help him anyway.

He had the upper hand. I really think he knew it. The only thing I had was that I was a good person. I tried to be anyway. In the end he decided to tell me. Not, I think, because he was afraid. I believe he told me knowing that he would get another chance to kill me. But he also knew that I beat him easily the first time. The next time he would need to change things up significantly if he would have a chance.

"The traveler. The ancient one sent you here. He took the gate-stone from you and sent you to die in the desert. Maybe you should ask, why did you foolishly align yourself with him? It doesn't matter though. The Master will find him as well. There is an old feud between them. The Master is not forgiving."

My next question seemed like the best one so far.

"How did you get here?"

"The artifact. It can send a person anywhere. It simply requires corruption to fuel it. An evil action to give it the power required," he replied.

"I won't give it the sacrifice it needs. And I think, there won't be anyone coming to offer you the chance to reactivate it." I knew the kind of evil action required to create corruption. Murder and death were the tools of darkness. I wanted no part in the thing.

I refrained from talking to the man again till I took my farewell. The sun had been down for less than a half an hour when I began walking toward the growing halo of light to the east. That halo was light from a city. I hoped it was Luxor. Though the walk was long, I had a great deal of time to think. It was nearly dawn when I came to the M75 highway and flagged down a passing truck. Quick conversation told me the driver was headed to Luxor. In fact, he was headed to the airport. He dropped me off at the hotel just after dawn.

I managed to convince the concierge to give me access to my rooms. I called Hector to let him know I was fine. He informed me that they'd reported me missing. The authorities had organized a search that would be starting that day. Several calls were required to cancel it.

I gathered the group and related the events in the desert. Though a great deal of potentially new information had been gathered, we decided to get back home and put the desert behind us.

It seemed like a sloppy metaphor. The desert of my imagination. I continued to be trapped in a world that I could barely control. I knew that control was an illusion. The best hope I had was that I'd somehow make a difference in the fight ahead. I knew that I had managed to survive against the odds. Maybe I was only meant to survive.

I thought about it for some time and realized that I'd not have the chance to do even that. The corruption that had slowly invaded my body would kill me long before the idea of being a survivor could matter. No, I was destined only to be a small chapter in the ongoing struggle. I realized I probably would not survive the next few years, let alone the war. I consoled myself knowing that I'd helped put a name to the evil we faced, Da Ra Cha Ti.

I thought about looking for the ancient ruins later but never got the chance. Events were transpiring faster than I'd imagined. Academic curiosity not only had to wait, it was not important.

A Champion

We had a few clues to the next step but without any solid leads we felt it would be best to return home and do some research. I remembered reading something about a connection between the Manandans and several other cultures in one of the family journals but still needed to confirm my suspicions.

Also, there were several questions I needed to answer. Such as who this third ancient being was and, although I took him at his word, why he felt I necessary to steal the geode from me.

His explanation that he wanted to escape the influence of Da Ra Cha Ti was, on the face of it, a reasonable excuse. I felt that there was an underlying truth that he had been unwilling to reveal. I also wondered exactly how he'd managed to transport me to the middle of the desert.

I was sullen and dejected the entire flight home. Though Nick, who sat next to me, offered the occasional distraction of conversation, I felt stupid for having let Dr. Ka-nas get the better of me.

Somehow this had not removed the feeling that he was on our side. Or at least we were both enemies of the same evil. Surely he must realize that together we stood a better chance of winning.

I remembered what I'd learned about these beings. They have great stores of power but because they do not have imaginations like normal people, they are powerless to create. Even though they seemed to understand the mechanics of creation, without this one emotional tool, they were unable to see beyond what was and imagine what could be.

In the end they were relegated to being teachers and guidance counselors. Da Ra Cha Ti could not create but could control those who possessed the ability. He used it to spread corruption. He used corruption to ensure his own power.

I began to think of Dr. Ka-nas as a sort of bystander. He'd stayed out of the war for as long as he could, knowing that he would paint a target on his own back if he tried to fight back against his onetime companion.

Then there was the final of these four companions. Who or what could that one be? Was there another ancient being that we might enlist in our cause? Perhaps another enemy to replace the one we now faced.

Every question spawned more questions. The only place I knew where I might find answers was in an old library that usually contained kernels of truth hidden in some allegory suited for a Sunday sermon. It was painstaking work but with Arianna's help, I felt like I might have a chance of actually getting to the bottom of at least a few of the questions before we decided on a new direction in our investigation.

Min had planned our return trip which included a three-day layover in LA. I wondered at her reasoning for the delay. Still my trust in the entire team was absolute. If she chose this plan of travel she had thought the matter through.

We were met at LAX by Min. She had recovered sufficiently to welcome us. As we waited for our luggage after having passed through customs, she explained the reason for our altered schedule.

She drove us to the north of the city in a large SUV. Along the way, she informed us of an interesting family relic which seemed to indicate a possible clue in our current investigation.

The Jade artifact had been hand carved during the early Shang dynasty. If her understanding of the bowl was accurate, it would have been created perhaps 1500 BCE. Along the edges of the bowl were carved what seemed like typical writing from the period. Below that was a dragon carved around the entire bowl.

The long thin scaled body wrapped the bowl several times. At each crossing of the body, either above or below, a medallion which seemed to be standard from the period was placed above the dragon's body. There were five of these and each represented one of the five elements in Chinese alchemy. Fire, water, wood, metal, and earth signs which also held an interesting set of lines above and below the medallion. It was these lines Min wanted to show us.

We arrived at a home in the suburbs north of the city. Though humble and somewhat moderate, the home had been modernized several times and small indications of the history of the home had been left to tell the complete story of its existence.

The stucco home had been built in the late sixties. Long narrow windows of clearstories were exposed just below the overhanging eaves. Where the home would have originally had clay tile roofing, a modern asphalt shingle replacement had been done sometime recently.

The owners had transformed the yard into a garden of drought tolerant foliage. Several trellises were inter wound with creepers and lightly colored flowers. Where there had once been a lawn, small gravel stones of a wide variety of colors now covered the remainder of the yard.

The front door had also been replaced with a custom door carved in a very traditional Chinese dragon and turtle motif. Min opened the door for us and bade us enter.

The interior of the home had been completely transformed. Although the walls remained intact, all of the furniture and decoration created the feeling of being in a Chinese restaurant. The living room floor was hardwood covered in several Asian rugs piled on top of each other. Along the walls stood sideboards with small statues of Buddhas and dragons. Three small couches stood along the walls. These were heavily lacquered wood with tapestry seats and backs. The dining area was separated by carved screen panels depicting a mountain scene.

As we were given the obligatory tour by Min, she introduced us to her grandfather Chun and father Jin and stepmother Lai, also her cousin Kun, who had a room in the converted garage.

Lai was the only woman in the home currently. One aunt had passed away and the others moved out recently. Her grandmother had died some time ago and her real mother disappeared not long after Min had been born.

We gathered around the black glossy table. At its center, the large bowl sat on a red silk pillow. The bowl was almost sixteen inches in diameter and ten inches high. The dragon relief was carved about a half inch deep at the most. The detail was amazing. Min pointed to each medallion and the corresponding marks above. These seemed almost to be deep scratches in the flat areas above and below the circles. They might have been added at a later time.

Above the symbol for fire, the scratches seemed oddly familiar. As though I'd seen the shapes they formed in a dream. A long horizontal scratch was topped with several lines that seemed to jut up at slightly different angles. Near the base of the sketch were three lines forming an obtuse triangle which corresponded to the formation of the rift gate.

The marks above the medallion for water had an interrupted horizontal with a slightly curved line starting near the left most and curving down into a vertical. The triangle was just to the right of the downward sloping line.

For earth the symbol seemed to be a rough rounded object with the triangle in the center. Now I began to understand. The mark here would have been the shape of the geode when it was intact. These marks must indicate the five primary gates. The first was the crack in the basement of the Drakson home. The second the waterfall entrance in New Mexico. I looked at the others and recognized the temple in Asia.

That left the final one which seemed to be a slight upward curved line with an eye shaped sketch below. The symbol which I now took to be that for a rift gate was within the eye.

This new clue was the next best lead we had. The problem was it indicated several lines which could correspond to any number of things or a wide variety of places.

"Do you think this last symbol relates to a place?" I asked the gathered team.

"It is very likely. Since all of the locations with the exception of the geode are found within the earth, and the geode is made of earth, I'd say we think about locations such as caves and the like," Arianna offered.

"I agree," Min added. "There is also this."

She motioned for us to inspect a large lacquered cabinet which stood along the wall adjoining the kitchen. There was a scene in gold and red inlay on the front panel. This showed a line of a cliff. Near the base of the cliff several geometric steps wandered into the sea. Just above these was the sign of the rift exactly as it appeared on the bowl.

"Is that the Giants Causeway?" asked Hector. We turned to him as a group and smiled.

"What? I got an A in geography," he smiled knowing that we were not questioning his interpretation, simply agreeing with him. "Really, ask Lucy."

Dinner was a variety of vegetables in a rather salty sauce with rice and noodles. The quantity offered filled our bellies. The conversation remained focused on our adventure.

Min's father, Jin, had told us of the family tradition that once every second generation a new child would be chosen to be the guardian. Min was the only child of her generation and the selection process that would normally have occurred had been bypassed. Thus at an early age, she'd begun to train.

The gate that the family guarded was one of the lesser gates. It had been covered over by a lake in the late seventies when a dam had filled the valley which had been the family home.

The family maintained the tradition even though they were in essence a family without a cause. The patriarch had insisted that Min might be needed for some other purpose and began her training even though she'd been born a decade after the family left China.

Many of the basic techniques that he'd taught her were applicable in everyday martial arts anyways. There were also hidden solutions to several of the movements she'd learned. These were meant to attack creatures of corruption. Several others were movements designed as spell components.

The one area of her training that he'd been unable to complete until recently was related to utilizing a gateway as a tool. Certain techniques would enable the user to see into the world and locate evil. Others might allow the user to see possible futures. The main use was to travel to any source of evil and corruption and stop it from completing whatever its plan might be.

To explain the difference between a primary gate and one of the twenty or so minor contact points is somewhat difficult but the basic is that, a primary gate is a focus point for energy as well as mentality. A simple allegory might be the difference between our eyes and our skin. With our eyes we can interpret a huge amount of information as it is one of our primary senses. Our skin has thousands of nerve endings which allow us to feel the world around us but the information is less conclusive. Maybe that isn't exactly correct but the idea, I think, is sound.

The primary gates are Grieta's eyes and ears in our world. They are also conduits of power which can be used to control all the other gates, thus if we control those five, we can lock access to all of them.

The secondary gates still allow contact but less intense and more subtly. The forces of corruption can use them to transfer mentalities into host bodies or even physical entities to our world. All access to them is funneled through one of the primaries though.

It made sense that the daggers of Thane, the bowl, and the many other artifacts we'd come across had elements that reflected the five elements, the five points of the pentagram, and other metaphysical symbols that seemed to have their basis on the function of these contact points to the mentality which was Grieta. This was the only known way to travel between worlds.

We'd also discovered that navigating the rift was not easy in any way. The mind projects its own understanding of the rift. There is a very real dream realm that changes as quickly as the imagination of the mind that is interacting with the rift. You bring your own failings and problems but more importantly, you bring your own fears. These are made real in the rift. While traversing, strict mental discipline is the only way to ensure a peaceful passage.

I'd read in the Drakson journals how the environment inside the rift was not conducive to human life. This was strictly due to the power of human imagination to create hostile events. Fear was the enemy.

We now had a possible location for further investigation. Many of these ancient cultures had had contact which seemed to defy the distances and technology of the time. I was finally understanding the totality of interconnection of the various groups that interacted with Grieta in the past.

It also made sense that the Drakson family, though well versed in some elements of rift lore, had such a negative view of Grieta when I'd first met them. They'd come into contact with the rift through the Manandan culture which had been decimated during the war between tribes in the area. Much of the secret lore had been lost.

Finally, we had begun to not simply reconstruct the knowledge that had been lost, but to expand on it enough to be of considerable aid in our fight against evil.

Power for Spells

Min asked me to join her at the family Xuéxiào. This was a martial arts studio that her grandfather started as a way of providing the family an income while still being able to pursue the more important aspect of tradition.

The large building was built in a modern style but the façade had the appointments of an early Chinese Buddhist temple. The interior consisted of a large front practice room adjoining a smaller personal training area in the rear.

The wood panels that separated the rear from the main area were carved in artistic traditional martial arts scenes as well as peaceful mountain settings. These were carved through so that the scene would be opposite from the other side however there was a soft red silk liner that backed the panels blocking the view between the two rooms of the school.

Along the walls stood racks of weapons made of black and red lacquered wood. Panels along the side walls showed proper techniques by way of traditional paintings with the name of the posture written under in the older traditional Chinese.

Along the back wall was a raised dais. The wall behind this was covered in several scrolls showing the lineage of Min's family going back some twenty-five generations. This was in the form of a simple list. Min and her husband Hector held the last entry at the far lower left of the wall. I had the impression that the entire thing would be rewritten once the next heir came of age and married.

In the center of the dais stood a large oak chair with a heavy red cushion seat. There sat Min's grandfather. He silently looked on while she ran me through the forms she taught me.

"These postures are used for generating internal energy. The power of Chi can be created by using emotional force. To access it, one must simple breath in, and focus on the required emotion enough for it to come into the heart. Then release it for the intended purpose." She drew in a breath and held it for a moment. I saw a look of anger come into her eye. She moved swiftly as she breathed out a long and frightful yell. Her hand came down hard and seemed to slam into an invisible object in a hammer fist. She had slipped into a square stance. Her left arm was cocked in an "L" shape, above her head. The right fist stood unmoving straight in front of her.

"Now the power is spent. You must breath in and restore the energy by drawing the force from your center. Here. Just below your navel. This is called the Dian Tien. This is the place where all the meridians of power flow through your body." She touched me just under my belly button. "Now you," she insisted.

I tried to repeat the movement as I'd seen her do it. She shook her head and reminded me that skill was not always about performing the movement correctly but also about the feeling of force and emotion I could generate. She asked me to try again but to remember for just a second the time I felt the angriest.

This time I could feel the well of anger build as I struck downward with the fist. She nodded as did her grandfather.

She continued to show me movements to elicit a variety of energies from whatever emotion I could. The most powerful emotions generate the most effective energy. Generally, they would take a greater time to recover when utilized.

There seemed to be a major drawback as well. The more a person utilized the more negative energies, the more a person would fall to the overpowering effect of its emotion. Anger generates more anger. Hatred and fear and negative emotion are traps as well as sources of power.

If a person became adept at using these, that person would constantly generate corruption which could be harnessed for evil purposes. In fact, it was known that Da Ra Cha Ti could draw on these powers from the user and turn them against you.

On the other side of the scale were the powers of joy and love. These could create lots of power too but these energies could only be used to create, not destroy. To heal instead of harm. The same potential problem would occur. A person could easily become addicted to these feelings and later be unable to defend themselves due to the desire to do only positive things. The feelings of anger might not even be possible anymore.

So balance was the answer. Each time negative power was used then a balancing positive power should be employed. Though the overall level of energy available would never be as great as from a person devoted to one method, the person would never fall into the trap of not having the right power when needed.

Min had studied how the garments of the Drakson family had been constructed and concluded that the long process of weaving the spells into the fabric could be bypassed by drawing the needed component from the rift itself.

While in the rift, the mind creates what it imagines. Hector had created a chrome plated pistol capable of blasting corrupted creatures to dust while in the rift. I'd actually summoned Kayle's short sword as well. I had the idea that once something had been created it could be summoned from the rift. So if that were true then a spell created while someone was in contact with the rift might then be attached to a physical object such as a shirt.

After several hours of studying, I had become exhausted and needed some time to rest. Min had also expended a great deal of energy and though she'd recovered nicely, she was still somewhat weak compared to her normally athletic and energetic disposition.

We decided to reconvene the next morning when she would bring the geode half she'd been given charge to protect. We could test the theory about the spells then. In the meantime, I would develop a series of them that would draw upon the emotional energy she'd explained and prepare them for conversion into my garments.

I began by considering the kinds of spells I would probably need. Some attack and defense spells and perhaps a few for healing. I thought some kind of smoke screen or confusion spells would be useful as well. Finally, I felt that several spells that might enhance my senses could be of benefit.

I mentally went over what Min had taught me earlier. Through the motions of the healing exercise I'd been using to minimize the effect of the corruption that was slowly killing me, I could insert emotional context and therefore draw energy for use in the spells. The forty-eight postures of the style I'd learned could each be modified slightly for my purpose.

I felt as though I could construct the effect portion of each spell on the fly so I focused on the foundation of each spell. I wanted them to be quick and easy to perform. This gave me the idea that all components would be similar making it simpler to produce the spell. The downfall would be that they would be easier to defeat once an opponent understood the mechanism they had in common. I was willing to risk that knowing that I could prepare several more spells in the limited time I had available.

For the attack spells, I prepared two that were simple explosive energy blasts. Each had slightly different effects. One was local to a small area and very powerful while the other had a radius of about ten feet and though less powerful, would cause a great deal of damage to several creatures in a sort of area effect.

I also adapted one I'd used before that forcefully expulsed corruption from a physical form. This took a great deal of energy and I felt compelled to use anger as its basis of power.

The final attack spell I created was meant to attack the mentality possessing a physical form. We'd seen that the mind had to draw energy of its own from living bodies or from the residual corruption left over from a horrible and evil action. The spell would disconnect the mentality from its power.

For defense, I felt I should have several barrier spells ready. I built some that were area effect and many that were simply shields against a single attack. When we first fought the corrupted corpse of Mathias Drakson, Maria and Jamas has used a globe shaped warding that prevented a corrupted creature from crossing. I added that spell to the list as well.

Healing spells were always a premium. These I knew could be invaluable so I created several versions. Some that would be more physical and others that would offer some mental respite.

I'd made glamour and confusion spells before and these were also in the mix. I was pretty good at them so I created the formulae for several types including dazzle, smoke and maze configurations. These would either force the mind to follow the path in the maze or simply bewilder the mentality with lights or diminished ability to sense the world.

After having developed these and the enhancement spells, I rested. It had gone past midnight when I'd finished and though I felt exhilarated, I was also exhausted.

In the morning I woke to Min knocking heavily on the door. We walked the two blocks to the family Xuéxiào. As we traversed the quiet in the early morning, we talked about the coming experiment. The spells, if successfully created would add to our general understanding of how the rift worked. It could also mean a real shift in the war against Da Ra Cha Ti.

Min seemed excited. Her demeanor was both buoyant and contagious. I felt a smile creeping across my face as she enthusiastically reiterated the instruction she'd offered from the day before. I listened with a smile. Who was I to diminish the joy she felt knowing that she'd helped us move toward a potential end of the fight.

Inside I secretly worried. I knew this would work. I understood the principles as well as anyone. I'd done my homework and my confidence in this particular exercise was not questionable.

My worry was that it wouldn't matter. We'd come so far and each time we'd somehow managed to survive. We diluted ourselves thinking that we were winning. I was afraid that we were actually simply delaying the inevitable.

Our enemy had been planning for thousands of years. Lifetimes had come and gone and still humanity was threatened. Perhaps we'd only stayed the hand of fate. With the end game in sight, we tried as hard as we could and we would probably still fail. That was my fear anyway.

But Min was smiling and it made me smile. I thought about my preparations and knew that this particular moment would not be one that ended in failure.

I could give hope where there was none. I could give the impression that we could win. For my friends and family, I could lie and say that all was ok. I would perpetuate the illusion of impending victory. Maybe that was all we had, an illusion.

Once at the Xuéxiào, Min and I activated the gateway and the overpowering feeling of joy filled my heart and soul. I felt the proximity of that which I'd come to love and cherish. To me Grieta had once been simply an artifact of the ancient universe. She had become the center of my hope.

Together Grieta, Min and I built the spells. They appeared magically on the fabric of the shirt that I'd prepared. I knew that when I spoke the keyword and made the proper motions, each spell would activate and the effect would become reality.

After nearly ten hours of focused concentration, I fell into a deep sleep.

When I woke up I continued for several more hours. Always I was in contact with the rift. Min stood by me as I persevered through the creation process. Here in contact with the rift, I could create what I imagined. I had it perfected. Each thought was ordered. My creations would be exactly as I'd designed them to be.

The real terror of the rift is the uncontrolled mind. A stray thought would create something that could be as evil as any devil we imagined. Focused and functional thoughts could create detailed elements which, when combined with the right power, would be formidable.

Once completed, I retired to the back area of the Xuéxiào. I don't know how long I slept. I knew that when I awoke, I would be forced to take the next step in the campaign against the darkness. I needed to find Dr. Kanas and retrieve the other half of the geode.

The Third Ancient

I was worried that finding Dr. Ka-nas would not be easy. He had centuries of experience avoiding detection. My first instinct was to let him go. The problem was I felt he'd be vulnerable to corruption and that the geode he possessed would fall into the hands of Da Ra Cha Ti. For no other reason than that, I needed to locate him quickly.

We'd known that the two halves of the geode were attuned to each other. They acted as though they were the same gateway. When using one you might inadvertently be transferred to the other. That had happened when Hector and I had entered the rift to repair the damage done by corruption. We went in though one half of the geode and exited through the other. With that in mind, I thought one way of potentially finding him, and therefore it, would be to use the one in our possession. I wanted to have as much backup with me as possible so I asked Nick to join me for the attempt. Min and Hector would act as anchors for the rift opening locally while Nick and I transited the gate.

I'd been working on a method for using the two as a sort of teleporter for a quick method of travelling between locations. I had even though of using the local gates for that, making a kind of transportation network that would allow for quick access between wide distances. What remained for us to do was catalogue as many of the gates on earth as we could.

By pointing that out, I hope to show both how difficult it would be to do and yet at the same time how far I'd taken the theory. So far I'd only used the gates for transportation a few times. I still felt the gates were less predictable than conventional travel.

I felt like I was worrying over nothing. The fact that I enjoyed a friendship with the mentality that was the rift, meant that it should be an easy transition. There were a great number of variables though. The largest concern at the onset was Nick.

He'd never been through the rift. I knew that his nature was calm and controlled but I could imagine that his subconscious mind might harbor fears and violence. I would want to coach him about passing through the rift in order to reduce the chance of accidentally creating something that could be dangerous for us.

"The thing you want to do is imagine positive things, flowers meadows and the like. Peaceful images should fill your mind. More important, they should fill your heart. It sounds a little weird I know but it's where creation comes from. We create with our imagination and emotion linked," I told him. "Just imagine the things that make you the most happy or peaceful."

"Sure, I can do that," he said calmly. Nick was never very verbose. I'd learned that he communicated with actions instead of words.

"Are you sure?" I asked. I mean it's not as easy as you might think and..."

"Yeah. I get it. Feel good, not bad. Look, I know I'm just a big hulk to you but I can act pretty well. Drama in high school you know," he offered as a friendly rebuttal.

I wondered if that would work. I guess it really didn't matter. We were planning on trying in just a short time and if Stanislavski's or Strasberg's "Method" worked for him then it didn't matter. So I accepted his affirmation and moved on to the basic plan.

"We don't know where he is or what he has prepared for us on the other side so be prepared to jump back into the rift quickly even if it means we give up the chance to get the geode back," I continued. "Once we are through, we'll need to determine the best plan of action quickly. If it turns out to be a fight, then I'll leave it to you to undertake the heavy lifting. I'll do my best to trap and contain him while you move in to subdue."

"I can use the lens I've got to do a little looking before we get there but the information will probably be somewhat limited. I'll do that just before we transition from the rift to whatever location he is in. That way he will have less time to react if he realizes we are spying on him. We can make the final plan of action quickly and then slip through."

"Ok." He seemed to be completely comfortable with the general lines of the plan. "I want to say just one thing though," he went on. "You are more important to the fight we have than me. You should let someone else go. Hector or Arianna, since Min is still not fully recovered. I think it's important to the cause that nothing happen to you."

"If I die tomorrow," I paused. "I die. The fight goes on. Soon it will happen anyway. I can't fight it off forever and I'm getting weaker and less capable all the time. All of you on this team are important. You are all the family I have. I need to do this. I think, with me, we have the best chance. I think I should be the one because I want to and that means something. I need to continue to feel alive in order to be alive. Most of all, I need to do this because it is what I am supposed to do. I'm not any more important than any other person on this crazy planet."

"Ok," was all he said in return.

We gathered in the back area of the Xuéxiào. A wood block table had been set up in the center. Min's family and the team gathered in a rough circle around the geode which sat in a position of honor on a silk pillow in the center of the table.

I looked into the eyes of each of those gathered. First one then the next. Anticipation and belief shone from each face. I realized that they were counting on me to lead them. Maybe Nick was right. Maybe it was simply the thought of someone to lead them that was needed. I knew that before I died I would have to pass the torch. I felt more responsibility than I had ever felt before.

I'd had responsibility. Until I'd met the Draksons, I'd never taken it in any other way than a sense of duty. I did what I did because I must. Now the tide had turned and I felt the weight of each life. Not only those here but somehow I felt the burden of all human life. We must succeed or there would never be freedom. Perhaps Da Ra Cha Ti would simply remove the threat and end the lives of any creature that could create. The weight seemed to increase at that thought. I hoped I would not break under the strain.

I lifted the small metal disc from beneath my shirt. It hung on a silver chain from which depended a second charm of crystal in a gold hoop. I cleared my mind and said the spell while focusing on the geode.

"Let me see through you. This metal is the same as your metal and they are in harmony. I can see through the mirror I create."

A light began to pulse in the crystal formation at the center of the geode. It was dim at first but quickly grew to be as bright as light bulb. The color of the light was slightly green and blue giving the room an eerie quality.

I felt contact with the mind of the rift. Joy and happiness swept over me in wave after wave of emotion. I could tell from the faces of those gathered that they too felt emotion stirring from contact with Grieta.

"Hello," the friendly voice contacted our minds. "I'm happy to be with you again my friends. Nǐ hǎo Lǎoshī," I could tell she was addressing Min's grandfather. They must have known each other long ago. Perhaps when he was the guardian of the gate in China.

No one else spoke but Grieta knew our purpose. She was quite literally connected to our minds at that point. Without waiting for us to prepare, she swept Nick and I into her mind and set us on our way.

I felt her say that she wished me luck as the world fell away and we found ourselves on a plain of grass where there were no trees or other signs of vegetation. The horizon was exactly horizontal. My mind and Nick's mind had come up with similar references for projecting our interpretation of the mentality of Grieta.

"Where do we go from here?" Nick asked.

"We should be able to simply return through the contact point that we came through and return to the other geode. Simply focus on that for now while I prepare the lens again," I offered. We turned to look at the green and blue halo of the contact point though which we had just been drawn. It seemed like a sort of aurora which shifted slowly in ribbons of color.

I placed the lens up to my eye like a monocle from a mystery movie set in the nineteen thirties England. Looking back at the gate, I saw the outline of a small chamber. Within, I could see the geode. Details were fairly sketchy but I knew that at that moment the ancient man we came to know as Dr. Ka-nas was not in the sphere of my senses. That didn't mean he wasn't there.

I told Nick what I was seeing.

"The only thing for it is to go through," he said. "If he isn't there and we have a chance to get it without conflict then we should try."

I agreed. We stepped through together.

As the ribbon of gauzy green film parted, I could see the room clearly. It seemed to be an apartment in North America. The American food stuff on the counter and the soda bottle on the table gave evidence of that much.

The table was a laminated top with a band of chrome wrapping the edge. Four mismatched chrome tube chairs had been pushed under and out of the way. One window looked out over an urban setting and the door opened into what seemed to be a living area.

At the center of the table stood the geode. It seemed unguarded. With no Dr. Ka-nas in sight, I confidently stepped forward and palmed the rock.

As I held it closer for inspection I heard his voice from the other room.

“Come in gentlemen,” he said rather genially. “It is time we talked.”

“I cannot imagine what we have to talk about,” I said loudly. I decided it would be discourteous to not hear him out so I stepped through to the living room.

He sat in a large leather chair with an arched back and rolled armrests. He seemed to be enjoying a cartoon on the older style television. A smile crept over his face as he continued.

“I cannot understand the need of the creature in the show to try and capture that bird. Every time it fails. Yet, it tries again. It has such imaginative ways of trying and yet for all its intelligence and creativity, it fails. I wonder if you realize how much like that you are?” he asked.

"Maybe I'll fail. But if I don't try we all fall to corruption. That isn't something I'm willing to allow. If I even have the smallest chance to stop it, I must try. I will use any imaginative or creative way I can think of to do just that," I tried not to be indignant but his manner seemed almost patronizing.

"I still need the geode to escape this world when Da Ra Cha Ti comes. He will try to destroy me as well. He feels I've been tainted by evolved life. He believes I might somehow become a creative power too. That I might have learned the secret of imagination," he sighed. "Alas I fear that is beyond me."

"Then we might be your only hope," I extended the branch. "If you help us we can be more prepared for whatever he does. We are stronger together. Our ability to create and your understanding of the universe could be a powerful combination."

"That was tried before. Be Got Si Ti tried to aid people in the war against him. He found out and devised a way to end the existence of my companion. Those people were so much better prepared than you are. They spent lifetimes perfecting their powers. Yet still he won. Still they died. Soon I will too. Unless I get away. I can at least try to convince him that I'm not a threat by staying out of this. I can try," he responded.

"Why haven't you jumped away yet? You could be half way across the universe by now," Nick wondered aloud.

"I cannot transfer through space in this form. If I do I will be trapped in it till I find another to accept my mentality. The mind of the rift will not let me move out of this body and back to the formlessness I once enjoyed. There is a barrier that keeps me contained." The explanation was obvious but he had the details wrong.

"It isn't the rift that keeps you trapped. That is the power of the spell that Zach placed upon the gate. I extended it to the geode and the rift locations we already have discovered," I informed him. "Once we have the last of the primary gates we can control access against anyone."

"I guess you have thought of everything," Dr. Ka-nas smiled. "Still I won't let you take that."

"You can't stop us," I said forcefully. "But, you can join us."

"No I can't," he said as he rose from the chair. "Now it is time for you to feel the full power of an ancient."

He raised his hands and pointed them at me with the fingertips stretched toward me like spears.

Instinctively, I put up a barrier spell which disappeared from the collar of my shirt.

The force of the blast of energy was tremendous. I buckled under the weight of the power which he had unleashed. Somehow my spell was holding and I concentrated enough willpower of my own to keep it from failing.

I decided not to try any attacks on the off chance that I could still change his mind. I had a spell of confusion that I hoped would work. It was a kind of stun spell that befuddled the mind as though heavily intoxicated. It included the nausea one sometimes gets when over drunk as well. I let it roll off of my sleeve and smiled as he staggered backward into the wall.

His force of energy vanished instantly and he fell to his knees and began to dry heave. I moved forward, continuing to concentrate on the spell.

When I was within a few feet I asked him, "Shall I stop? Will you relent?"

He nodded while still coughing and gagging.

I let the spell fade and nodded to Nick to help him up. Nick gave him an arm and he slowly rose to his feet shaking off the effects of the spell.

"You could have killed me," he seemed confused. "Why didn't you?"

"No need. We have what we came for. I still hope you are willing to help in our fight. If not...," I let the sentence drop as I shrugged.

I didn't want him to think I was desperate for his assistance. I knew that we stood a better chance with him if only because he knew the enemy personally. To have that sort of insight would be invaluable.

"Ok," He said after a long sigh.

Prometheus

We returned through the rift to California. It had been decided that we would remain there for another few days while we conversed with Dr. Ka-nas. Once we learned as much as we could we would plan for the next stage in our journey.

Dr. Ka-nas was ready to discuss his past association with Da Ra Cha Ti in detail. He warned that we might not understand much of what he had to say. None of us had the frame of reference for being an entity without form. Time for the ancients was simply another way of measuring. For people, time was a clock that ticked away the hours and seconds of our lives.

I was surprised that he used such a metaphoric phrase for human life. There is creativity in the use of language. This was something he'd obviously learned over the millennium of his life.

I wondered the difference between creativity and imagination as it related to the magic within the universe. Somehow I knew that the answer was probably beyond me.

Dr. Ka-nas obliged by explaining the difference between creativity and creation. Knowing that there is something beyond reality is one thing. The ability to believe in that which is without foundation is strictly a trait of those creatures which know the passage of time. We can imagine then create through belief.

A being such as an ancient can think of things beyond the real world but cannot believe in anything beyond the boundaries of the physical and metaphysical universe. They can use the power of the universe in a raw and unformed way. Only those with the power of belief may create.

Ka-nas told me of the beginning of time as he remembered it.

He was once a spirit of the universe. For much time he wandered alone. During this memory, he did not measure time. He witnessed the beginning of the stars and the planets around those stars. Then he saw the seeds of life begin upon the faces of the worlds.

It was then he encountered the other two. Be Got Si Ti and Da Ra Cha Ti. They said he was one of their kind and named him, Mi Cal La Sa.

Da Ra Chi Ti means the first of those who are found. Be Got Si Ti means the one who understands. Mi Cal La Sa is the one that defends the truth.

They met another during their journey together. This one was called Ka Lia Ma Lan which is the one that lights the darkness. The fourth of the ancient beings saw the universe as an evolving, changing, and dynamic place. With each age that passed, new life and light came into existence. For many ages the four enjoyed watching the ever changing and always evolving worlds where people had begun to dream.

Be Got Si Ti watched the first act of creation. It was a little girl who saw the stars and wished to journey among them. This wish opened a gate between worlds. It was the first time the four became aware of the rift.

The four studied the process of creation and attempted to create but though they could imagine, they could not believe.

By this time the four had also begun to understand emotion. They'd watched people react unpredictably and thought the behavior was interesting. One by one they experimented with having emotions of their own and found the practice exhilarating.

The problem was simple though, they could feel and therefore they could fear. They understood creation but could not practice it. In an effort to protect themselves they decided they should guide the young races so that they would not use the power of creation to destroy.

The evolutionarily young species accepted the ancients as guardians for some time. Many worlds were visited and at each contact rules of use of creativity were given to the cultures. Those cultures that were of a violent nature were taught to have compassion. The hope was that the power of creation would benefit the universe if not simply the individual races.

Humans became aware. They began to imagine. They began to create. In innocence they lived and died and all the while they did as they needed to guarantee the survival of their own race.

Be Got Si Ti was the one that began to teach humanity the ways of creation. It was he that realized that man created corruption when the act of hate or anger was done. He was afraid of the pervasive power of corruption. He knew that corruption destroys. In its wake the fabric of the universe slowly decays. It is like a disease that cannot be cured.

Some of these young races could only create in limited ways. Shapeshifting or seeing the past was very common. Humans and a few other races had limitless ability to create.

The companions knew that even though they'd been teaching the young races, there was a chance that they might grow beyond whatever instruction they'd received and begin to wonder whether they could do more.

It was Da Ra Cha Ti that first began to teach the young races to war. He figured they could destroy each other and that would be the end of it. When he discovered that violence on such a large scale created corruption on an equally large scale, he was initially afraid. Somehow he'd found that he could control corruption. The other companions never knew what sparked his discovery but this made them afraid of him. Slowly they drew plans to safeguard themselves and the young races against him.

Given a warning that Da Ra Cha Ti intended to begin a war on the youthful race of humans on earth, Be Got Si Ti took several families through the rift and deposited them on another world. There they flourished and build a great civilization. The success of this inspired him to seed many worlds with human life in hopes of saving them from eventual extinction.

The people of earth itself were spared because Da Ra Chi Ti had discovered his companions had turned away from him. Though confident, he knew he could not face them openly. He retreated for a time to consider his next move.

Da Ra Cha Ti had discovered that a mind could be extracted from a physical form and placed in another body by transferring them through the rift. He began to use agents to infiltrate worlds, allowing him to move quietly and unseen by his companions.

In experimenting with the possessions, he found that a mind could ride hidden in the background without the host even being aware of it. The possessing mind could also act in a symbiotic way with the host. The most startling effect was that a host mind could be overpowered and essentially absorbed by the parasitic mind. When this happened, the host mind was subverted to the will of the possessing mentality and could even be destroyed.

The final realization came when a possessed body that had died for whatever reason remained active for a time. Controlled by the invading mind, it could exert control over the body and reshape it somewhat. The limiting factor was the length of time the body would be utilized before its nerves and brain rotted enough to be unable to conduct the thoughts of the possessing mind.

He realized that a mind within a living body might be subject to the limitations of life. To put it another way, the mind would die with the body. In order to test his idea, he allowed the other ancients to learn the secret. Then he patiently waited for his chance.

The other ancients began enjoying occasional contact with people via possession. Though they would allow the mentality within the host body to remain active, they'd discovered that it would be easy to accidentally crush the mind of the possessed. After a time, it became natural for them to interact with people via a prepared volunteer. These people were considered by their own cultures to be sacred and sometimes godlike.

Millennia passed before Da Ra Cha Ti decided it was time to extract revenge for betrayal by seeding a war on the first people that Be Got Si Ti had aided in their escape.

The war on the other world lasted a hundred years and in the end the planet was laid barren. A family was rescued from that world by Be Got Si Ti before the final collapse. In order to safeguard them from the wrath of their enemy, he sent them to what we now call the second world.

Our planet, Earth, had been spared the direct attack that had destroyed the other world. Here Da Ra Cha Ti felt a slower, more deliberate tactic was needed. Two main factors forced this technique. The first was that the three had instructed several of the people of the world on how to defend against corruption and the agents of evil. The second was a more pressing matter. The gateways on the world had become linked to five primary points. He could send his minions in one at a time through the secondary gates but whenever he managed to get a minion through they were invariable destroyed before they could sow corruption on a larger scale.

A planet wide group of protectors had sprung up under the tutelage of the other ancients. These groups had secured the five primary gates and made access to the world so limited that his followers had trouble communicating and acting on his behalf.

Direct action was required.

Da Ra Cha Ti tricked Be Got Si Ti into having a conference. He used a human mage to cast a corruption on the mentality of the ancient. This spell bound him to a human body that when destroyed, would end the long existence of Be Got Si Ti.

He used a similar technique to trap Ka-nas, whose real name was Mi Cal La Sa, in the body he now inhabited but was unable to kill him before he escaped and warned the fourth of the ancients to stay away.

Ka-nas was now looking for a way to extricate himself from the body he'd been trapped in and escape himself into the vast reaches of the universe.

As soon as the war started, Ka Lia Ma Lan disappeared. It was later discovered that Da Ra Chi Ti had tracked down and imprisoned her mind in a living body. There it would remain until the body died a natural death. This was the punishment for defying the will of Da Ra Cha Ti.

Though he described the events in more detail than I've written here, I felt I should focus on only the most important points. Also, I admit to over simplifying the conflict between the ancients themselves as it seemed to be something of a sibling rivalry the way Ka-nas told it.

The problem as I saw it was that no simple family dispute should cause the enslavement and deaths of countless millions. As I wrote that, I remember that much of our history has cases where disagreement between family caused centuries of strife.

Battle Cry

We gathered again at in the rear room of the Xuéxiào, this time to discuss the next move. It was time for Ka-nas to tell us the location of the last primary gate. I wanted the entire team there for planning after the revelation.

We stood in small groups around the room waiting for Ka-nas to speak. When he did, it seemed like the voice of a long lost uncle or a cherished friend from childhood. He no longer seemed to be a man fearful for his life. His countenance was not unlike a parent comforting a child.

"The crystal gate is in the north of Hibernia, the Fiodh-Inis, a final land on the edge of the world, you now call Ireland. This is the place where you will find destiny for it was also once called the Inisfalia, land of destiny. There you will go, and bring me with you. I will aid where I can." His words were not unlike hearing a sermon from a much respected pastor.

We'd had the idea that it might have been exactly that. Hector even saw the similarity between the symbols on the objects at Min's parent home as probably being the Giant's Causeway. So we had a place to look and confidence that we might finally be able to bring this chapter to an end.

My first thought was to simply book a flight and head off to Northern Ireland. There seemed to be a few problems with the idea, though. First, was that we seemed to need Dr. Ka-nas with us and he was obviously without his passport and ID so an international flight might prove something of a challenge. Second, there had been several attempts on our team during the current adventure and we had become aware that the enemy had its eyes on us. If we were to move quickly, we might avoid detection long enough to complete the spell of control on the gate.

Finally, there was the fact that we knew that every gate had at one time a group of protectors. It was entirely possible that these protectors were still very active in Ireland. The only one of the primary gates that had been lost to modern man was the one in New Mexico behind the waterfall. The others had been under the control of one side or the other for all of remembered history.

I was just about to comment on my thoughts when we heard the sounds of scraping and a sort of raspy breathing. These came from the main practice area of the school. We looked through the narrow opening to see what caused such a sound, knowing what must have caused it. The dais blocked our view through to the other room, however, and we were forced to draw closer to investigate.

Lucy was closest to the opening. As we all pressed forward, it became clear that there were several sources of the sound from the other room. I cursed that I hadn't any weapons with me other than the spells threaded into the fabric of my shirt.

Lucy just stepped into the opening when I heard her gasp. She fell backward and turned toward us. A large weal of red spread quickly across her stomach. I grasped her hand and drew her back from the opening and sent a barrier spell to settle just on the other side of the opening.

The others gathered in a semi-circle around the passage while I knelt at Lucy's side. She looked up into my eyes and smiled as a tear of sadness fell from my face. I don't remember feeling anything at that moment but I must have. I tripped over the first spell of healing and it went away lost to my stammering attempt.

I refocused my mind and tried again with another of the three I had woven into my shirt. This one took hold and I saw the wound close up and scab over. I knew that she was still not out of danger but I felt the desperate need to help the others knowing that the barrier spell would eventually fail without me continuing to feed it energy.

I smiled and asked her if she would be ok. She nodded and closed her eyes. A small smile creased her face. I gently settled her head to the floor and stood.

As I turned I realized that the barrier had already fallen and agents of corruption had begun the active attempt to breach our defense.

Min and Hector stood to one side. Min's father and grandfather stood opposite of her. Each was engaged with a corruption creature. It seemed a ridiculous fight as the highly disciplined martial artist battled the reanimated bodies. Hector had obviously been practicing as he held his own against one of the creatures.

A small arc of the others remained in almost the same position as when I'd last looked. Nick and Agent Jermyn had drawn their side arms and were waiting for clear shots. Ka-nas stood near the center but simply stood with his hands at his side as though waiting for something. Arianna stood near the rear wall, her mouth hung open in an aspect of sheer terror.

Min had broken one creature down using a series of hand movements from the crane style which seemed to weave a spell that blasted corruption from the body on each contact. After several heavy blows, the thing fell to the floor and the sprinkling of glitter floated in the air where it once stood for a moment before wisping away on an unfelt breeze.

Min's father used a similar technique with the same result. Her grandfather seemed more adept at the technique and had dispatched two already.

Hector seemed less effective though he managed to keep his opponent at bay. I tossed a separation spell at the one he was fighting, allowing him a moment of respite while waiting for the next creature to advance.

Occasionally the flow of the fight would allow another creature to enter the fray. It almost seemed as though Min and her family had the entire fight planned so that they could manage each creature as it came through.

On the rare occasion that one got past the first line of fighting, Nick or Agent Jermyn or both would end the intrusion with several shots to the head. In the first minute only two had been destroyed in this manner.

There was something standing just on the other side of the partition to the right of Min's father. I could see a giant menacing shadow move across the red silk. Just as I saw it, the panel burst open and showered the room with splinters and shreds of bright cloth.

Large heavy arms reached through the demolished panel and grabbed Min's father. At the touch, he seemed to whither. His body stiffened and the luster in his eyes was replaced with a blue white gloss. His facial skin shrank and dried as his lips stretched back revealing teeth yellowed from age. He fell to the floor landing with a heavy thump. A devourer!

This was a creature of terrible power. Min had faced one while it was still adjusting to our environment and managed to defeat it only with the help of the Dagger of Thane. We'd also encountered one while on the second world where I'd used the sorcery of the one called Piyamaradush to turn it against him. We had neither tool available here.

When a devourer comes into a new world it shape-changes till it finds a form that offers the most potential in whatever environment it encounters. The one on the second world looked like a large snake with arms and legs. This one seemed to be a cross between a gorilla and a spider. Its face sported the general appearance of a gorilla with a dozen lidless spot eyes.

It stood nearly ten feet in height. The long forearms seemed heavy at the apex of the elbow. The fists were the size of a football helmet. Eight appendages resolved to four arms and four legs. The barrel shaped human torso sported a large round belly and a heavy four lobed chest. The abdomen tucked back sporting four legs flipped up and back in the shape of a spider. Though large and round, each section seemed well muscled and thickly boned. It crept over the edges of the rough opening it had created in the beautiful panel partition.

It moved somewhat like a horse with the legs in opposition, two on one side coming together as the two on the opposite side moved apart.

As it advanced, I sent a spell of confusion its way hoping to slow it somewhat.

The spell caused it to look around for a second as though it had seen a thousand small sparkles of fireworks. It took the creature only that second to realize the spell was not causing it harm before the creature continued its advance.

Min stepped forward again and began a series of spinning kicks which were meant to throw it off balance in one direction, the direction of her grandfather.

He stayed his hand till the creature had taken the full count of Min's terrible attack. Then he began his own series of focused attacks. These resolved into a left and right punching series that seemed to create waves of concussion at each impact.

In the meantime, Hector, Agent Jermyn, and Nick continued to fire and fight relentlessly against the lesser threat of the dead possessed who continued to flow through the center opening between the rooms of the school. Each had dispatched a dozen by now and none had slowed their relentless vigil during the battle.

I turned my attention back to the devourer. Realizing that Min and her grandfather had the harder task, I decided to employ the most powerful spell I had created thus far in an attempt to shorted the battle.

This was essentially a demolition of corruption. I knew that control of a devourer could only be maintained through the use of corruption. If I blasted the center of corruption with every ounce of energy I possessed, I felt I should be able to remove whatever mechanism that had been used to draw it to our world.

Unlike most creatures, devourers can travel through the universe without the use of the rift. I knew that once free of whatever spell it had been bound by, it would try to return to its origin. The spell would destroy the organization of the connection with corruption and hopefully force the creature to return to its home.

The first effect worked as I planned. The secondary intent of the spell was not as successful.

The creature looked around for a moment as though startled. It seemed free to do as it pleased. It pleased to continue to devour.

It lashed out toward Min but she managed to step sideways. As it moved deeper into the room, it came in contact with Agent Jermyn and grasped her around the left leg with the same disastrous result as before. Agent Jermyn shriveled in a second to a husk of the woman she'd been before.

I sent a firestorm spell at the creature but it ignored the imagined flames as it sucked the life from our friend.

I realized I'd been thinking incorrectly. This creature was not a corruption. And now not bound by whatever spell held it, it was a natural force doing what any animal would do. It sought to survive.

I wondered if any spell I possessed would have an effect. In the world of Earth, spells can only effect a corrupted creature. If it was no longer controlled by corruption would any spell have an effect?

To test the theory, I blasted it with a pain spell that was not woven into my shirt. This cost me some emotional energy I'd not been prepared to lose but the effect was worth it. The creature howled and bucked backward away from me as pain ran through its body.

With that knowledge I was prepared to spend the most powerful spell I had. I uttered the word and motioned in a large circle, finishing with the palm of my right hand extending rapidly toward the devourer.

I could sense the wave of power that flowed from me. It formed a cone of light. The palm of my hand was the pinnacle and the creature's face the base.

It exploded in a fury of red and blue sparks. The entire form seemed dissolved into a firework that shook the school to its foundations. The creature stopped for a moment and looked for all the world like it was surprised as it disappeared amidst the shower of glitter that followed.

I looked around and felt a huge sense of exhilaration knowing we'd managed to defeat this powerful thing. Min and her grandfather stopped their activity long enough to realize that the corrupted creatures pouring through had not yet abated.

Hector continued to use the half dozen techniques that seemed to work for him while Nick fired and reloaded as the ebb and flow of the fight permitted. I hadn't realized how close the creatures had gotten to either before I said the keyword for a spell that shocked the remaining creatures to oblivion.

I fell to the floor pained and exhausted. The room seemed to reel in circles around me. I could not focus on the faces of my friends. As the world went black, I realized I'd overspent the power I'd needed to finish the battle. The truth of what Min told me earlier was more than evident. I forgot the world as my mind tried desperately to recover what energy it could.

Symbiosis

I awoke with the worst headache I'd ever remembered. I felt dehydrated and sore all over. As I tried to stretch my limbs, I discovered new pains in my joints as well. When I opened my eyes, a blinding light cast irregular shadows on the walls and ceiling. I heard a soft voice telling me to relax, lay back and rest. I stopped moving, closed my eyes and fell back to sleep.

I dreamt I was floating on a cloud of ideas. They seemed to me to encompass every thought that any person had ever had. There were imaginings and musings and wonderings of the mind. There were great inventions and beautiful offerings mingled with the most innocent thoughts of joy and love.

There was also hate and anger and depression and darkness. Where men and women had jealousy and the desire to take from others that which was not their right. Pain of separation and loss was woven into the joy of renewal. Bigotry and sexism and fearmongering seemed to be all too powerful.

I wondered if the people of the world really deserved to be saved from their fate. We'd created a world where corruption in both the metaphysical form and the real legal sense were pervasive and accepted. We murdered each other at increasingly alarming rates. Though the words had changed, we still enslaved the masses for the benefit of the few. There is more evil in the world than the one we'd been fighting.

Then I saw it. A small light of an idea. The joy that comes at the birth of a child. And there the light of a soulmate whose eyes draw you in and your heart melts. And next to that the power of a gift of love. Beside that the simple act of kindness on any corner of any city in the world. A smile at a stranger. Holding the hand of a child in comfort. The hugs of a reunited family too long apart.

There was happiness and joy at a concert where the music uplifted the crowd and gave them reason to dance. A sad song that reminds us of lost love. The great machine to help a person walk. The towering skyscraper and the architect who worked tireless hours to see it completed. Every great achievement of humanity reminded me that though flawed, we are all worthy of life. We are all worthy of freedom.

I would do whatever needed doing. For all the things that I wish humanity was not, I would still fight for them. Not because they did or did not deserve it. I could not be the judge of anyone other than myself. I would do as I must, because it is who I am. Maybe I fool myself to think that that is a virtue. It is not. It is a simple statement of solidarity. We are all flawed. So I do what I do.

The next time I awoke, I felt much better though I still had a low grade headache. Again I tested my limbs by slow stretches and found that the pain I'd encountered before had passed. I opened my eyes and found a twilight world where my senses were spared the shock of full daylight.

Sitting on a chair next to me was Lucy. Her head rested upon her chest in an aspect that indicated she was sleeping. Her hands were crossed in her lap. Though she leaned back in the chair, she seemed to be slumped forward due to the angle of her head.

I recognized the room as the one I'd been assigned in Min's family home. The menagerie of dark wood carved Asian animals gave the room a sense of perspective. Several shelves contained these effigies. The tops of the dresser and the window sill were lined with smaller creatures which seemed to smile at me from their perches.

As I looked around, I realized that some of the figures had been carved from jade. These gave a slightly altered hue which was glossy and green but of several shades, each imbued with its own characteristic color.

I decided to lay there for a while and rethink recent events. The fight had been terrible but I knew that we'd at least fended off the corruption for a time.

To what end, I was still unsure. After each fight I ran through the event as though I could have done it better or saved one of those that we'd lost. I was still questioning myself after all these years and still I had no answers other than, what if?

Those possessed corpses reiterated the fact that we faced an enemy which used these minions to keep from being directly involved. Da Ra Cha Ti could sit back from the relative safety of his own domain, and direct the battle. Sooner or later we'd have to face him either on our world or his.

I realized that as an ancient being, he really didn't have a home world. He was a child of the universe whose mind was as old as Grieta's. What kept him from coming into our world as Ka-nas and Be Got Si Ti had done? I decided it was fear. He feared being trapped in a human form. He knew that once made flesh, he would be vulnerable.

As a formless mind, he could wander and control without the threat of death. I began to realize that death was what he feared the most.

It's funny when I think of it that a mind as old as his would be afraid of something that was unnatural to it. But truthfully, life was not part of its existence either. To be alive implies eventual death. The most natural process of a living organism is that it is born, it grows, procreates, then dies. This is the cycle of life.

Da Ra Chi Ti may have emotion and sentience, but he has none of the characteristics of life. It made him an interloper. He interferes with life for his own ends. I couldn't imagine a thing of greater evil than that.

Another thought began to creep in and cause me a moment of amusement. I shuddered when I first learned of corruption and how it controlled the body of Mathias Drakson. Fear seemed to be a constant emotion during the first year and a half of the fight we'd waged. But now as I began to really understand our enemy, I no longer feared him. I only rarely felt the terror generated by a corrupted creature.

While our enemy had great fear of us, I had lost my fear of him. If there was no other sign of our impending victory, the lack of fear gave me hope. What else did I have? My normal pessimism seemed to be fading only to be replaced by a totally unfounded confidence in the people that I'd come to call family.

I thought back to the battle again and mourned the losses. We'd managed to defend against one of the deadliest creatures known but with the loss of Min's father and Agent Jermyn. I remembered that Lucy had been injured as well and wondered at her sitting vigil over me while I slept. I recognized the voice I'd heard earlier and knew it to have been hers. She must have been sitting there for quite a while.

"Lucy?" I queried. "Are you awake?"

Her head nodded once then she lifted her gaze gently in my direction.

"Chris. You are awake and feeling better." It was a statement not a question. "That is good. There is so much to tell you. I am sorry for the loss of your friends, though. I wish I could have helped more, though."

"How are you? How is everyone?" I asked tentatively.

"The others are well. I saw what happened and was forced to intervene on your behalf. Though the shell of the form was near death I was able to occupy her body so that I could affect repairs on you. This was several days ago. Now you have recovered your strength and I must beg you to do something. It will be harder than anything I've asked of you before. I'm sorry."

I recognized the difference between the expected accent and attitude of Lucy and that of the mind behind the rift. Somehow Grieta's mentality was now inhabiting the body of Lucy. How could that have happened? Normally someone would have had to access a gate.

"Lucy?" I asked.

"Her body died. I was forced to use the shell as a medium to escape the attempted power struggle with the Master. I am without my place in the universe. I am a singularity now. I am separate from the vastness."

"Grieta?" It seemed too obvious but I had to ask.

"Yes, it is Grieta," she said. "I could not repair the body of Lucy before the mentality died. I'm stuck here now. If I leave the body it will die and I cannot return to the rift that was."

"Is the rift is gone then?"

"No. Think of the rift as my body. My mind now resides here in the framework of Lucy. I have her memories and thoughts but she, that thing that was particularly her, is no longer and I am not sure if I can ever return to the rift. I seem to be bound to this body."

"The rift is empty. Da Ra Cha Ti will discover this soon enough and try to extend his mind into that which was me. It will be easy unless he is opposed. I cannot leave the body I'm in. The body would surely die. Also, I know now that my sacrifice was a single action. It cannot be repeated. As I said I'm now bound to this body. When it dies I will also die. I can extend it for a time. Perhaps a few hundred years. In the end though, I will be unable to repair it and it will no longer function. When this happens my mentality will fade to join the universe."

"It is fitting. It is right that I should finally be given the same gift as any human. That I should be allowed to end. I've spent my existence alone. In the reaches of the universe I've never known the joys of being human. Now I can truly appreciate those things which fade with time."

"The color of the sunset last night was amazing and beautiful. The scent of the flowers in the planters behind the house are overwhelming. The feeling of watching you while you slept. You who have already given so much. Is there any other thing which I might give to you before I tell you what must be done?" she asked.

In my heart I knew that what she was going to ask would be the end of me. I felt the darkness drift into my thoughts and understood for the first time what my destiny must have been from the beginning. My mother showed a real sadness when she told me I was bound for greater things. Indeed, my father had a stoic countenance with every lesson he taught.

The Draksons took me into their family and taught me the true nature of things. Lucy, Hector, Min, Jack, Ron, and all the others were like family to me. They lived and died for the same important reason. Here we were nearly at the end. I hoped, at the end. I somehow knew what I must do. At least the cancer wouldn't kill me.

"I have to go into the rift," I said. "I have to keep the evil from taking control of that place. I must become what you once were."

"Yes," she said softly. "It is more than anything that has ever been asked of anyone. It will not be easy. There is a loneliness which cannot be quenched. There amongst all of creation you will be alone. None may enter. None may understand, but perhaps me, the emptiness which is the existence of the rift. You must become that which I was."

"You contain the spark of creation. A human mind in the center of reality will prevent the mind of evil from overcoming that place. You must become the center," she informed me.

"I don't understand. You can't go back?" I asked.

"No."

"What will happen?" I continued to press.

"I don't know."

"Will I be able to get back? To return to my body? I mean, if I enter the rift, and you aren't in the rift, what am I supposed to do?"

"I am sorry I don't have an answer for you. This is beyond my experience. I cannot leave the body I'm in or I will stop existing. I will die. The mind that was here is gone already, though I have her memories. The rift is empty. It was, in a manner of speaking, my body. Now it is devoid of a directing intelligence. If Da Ra Cha Ti were to control the rift, there would be no way to stop evil from overcoming the entire universe. No world would be safe," she informed me.

We sat at a large oak table on benches in the pub where we'd booked lodgings. A few chairs made of stripped wood sticks and small log chairs had been drawn close to accommodate the team members that didn't fit at the table. Min's cousin was busy at the bar ordering tea and scones, which he presently deposited in the center of the table for all to enjoy. Lucy wandered the room sniffing the flowers in planters and touching things as though she'd only just become aware of the diversity of experience she could have in our world.

I supposed that it was true. Though she retained Lucy's memories, she had never experienced any of it for herself. She seemed almost childlike as she smiled at each new sensation.

Hector sat next to me and Min sat next to him. The other side of the table was taken by Min's grandfather and Nick. Arianna had dumped herself in one of the chairs nearby. Ka-nas had pulled his chair to the end of the table and sat, his elbows on the table and his head resting on his cupped hands. He seemed to be pondering his predicament.

We'd arraigned travel papers for Ka-nas through a connection in Min's family. Though I doubted it had been completely legal, I was unconcerned at this point. We needed him with us in Ireland and however we managed to get him there would have to be accepted.

As it was there had been no difficulty in travel. The long flight allowed me ample time to research the potential site. Lucy sat next to me during the flight. She'd nodded off a couple of times and let her head rest on my shoulder. Each time we touched I felt the sensation of pure peace just as it was when I was in contact with the rift. Her perpetual smile was contagious. After a time, I felt that I was as happy as I'd ever been.

We planned on heading out after breakfast. Two large vans had been rented for the purpose of transporting us to the edge of the causeway. Though I could have tried to enter the rift and seal it against Da Ra Cha Ti using the geode, the gate here in Ireland could still give his agents a way of accessing the rift. I was unsure what I might be able to do once I'd entered. We came here to lock this location as we'd done the others. After, I'd try to enter the rift and do as Lucy asked.

I asked her, Grieta not to tell the others of my potential attempt to secure the rift from possible takeover. She reluctantly agreed. I'm not sure why I felt it should remain a secret but I felt a growing concern over my friends. They should not bear the burden of my choice. I didn't want them to worry over me.

Ka-nas had not been to the place in centuries. Though he had an outstanding memory, the possibility of him finding the exact location from his memory seemed somewhat suspect. From what I could tell, he'd been slowly losing the ability to maintain the body he had been inhabiting and would eventually age and die just as a human does.

Due to the potential problems with his memory, we planned on slowly traversing the cliff face till we found a geology that might match the simple sketch from Min's family heirlooms. I was well aware that we might have to investigate several potential sites before we found the location we were looking for. As it was, this turned out to not be necessary.

The drive from our lodging east of Londonderry to the causeway was relatively short. Though the road was large for the area, it was still only one lane each direction. This necessitated the regular slowdown for whatever local traffic might be using it. Though only about twenty miles of road, it took nearly forty minutes to get to the causeway head road.

From there we climbed out of the vans and began to walk along the trail that led down to the bottom of the cliff. Here were the famous geometric columns that formed the beginning of the causeway. The distinctive hexagonal stones edged up the cliff face some and tapered into the water on the north Atlantic, creating what seemed to be a giant manmade stone path ending at the crashing waves.

A tall pointed hill stood above these pillars of stone creating a green backdrop to the grey vertical.

Some of the pillars had been worn down forming dish shaped bowls in the tops. Small pools of water in them added to the eerie and overpowering sense of smallness.

We walked along hoping to find a sign of where we needed to go. Occasionally we'd stop to consult the sketches and photos we'd brought of the symbols that served as our guide.

Lucy did not stop however. She continued walking right up to the edge of the causeway and turned to the east. She pointed in the direction of a small cliff perhaps a mile in the distance and smiled. "There," was all she said.

We gathered our team and walked back up toward the causeway head. From there we travelled over the low end of the pointed hill and to the left. This led us to another smaller trail and then to a much smaller outcropping of the geometric columns which disappeared into the shallow cliff face below.

The trail was narrow. One side was a nearly vertical drop into the chill waters some twenty feet below. The other side was made of the faces of these pillars which formed every feature of the visible terrain.

After some thirty meters, we found ourselves at an opening in the pillars. The crack was framed with evenly formed columns making it almost seem to have been purposefully built. The deep cave beyond sparkled with light being reflected by thousands of white crystal shapes crisscrossing the walls and floor of the edifice.

We entered. The overall shape of the chamber seemed to be similar to a larger scale version of the small geode we possessed. The rift gate was near the center. It appeared as darker purple crystal in the now familiar angled crack from upper right to lower left.

Unlike in the past, I did not feel the background presence of Grieta. To be sure, she was here inhabiting the body of Lucy. Instead I felt an emptiness. As though we were on the edge of a great open space. It felt void and without form.

I quickly set up the spells necessary to secure the gate. There would be little time once completed to determine the best method for entry. Before I'd gone into the rift by entering the mind of Grieta. The rift became a reflection of my own imagination as I tried to interpret the environment. I wondered what it would be like to enter the rift with no mind to create form and substance.

The others gathered around as I prepared the apparatus of the spell. These included the lens and a charcoal stick of special materials that would be used to etch the proper spell into the surrounding crystal.

The charcoal was infused with the remnants of the original tripod brazier that Zach had used to create the lens two years before. I'd managed to develop a technique to recreate the basis of the spell without the extensive mechanics. This amounted to simply connecting the spell through the gate at the Drakson home. The lens became a sort of master key for all the gates.

As I meticulously went through the ritual of developing the lock on the gate, the others stood watch. Though the chamber was rather large, it felt crowded when accounting for the many people who now occupied the space.

Occasionally a tourist would wander near and peer into the crack. Nick turned them back with a gentle lie saying we were conducting an experiment and we'd be done in a few hours. They could come back then to enjoy the chamber without our large party being in the way.

I'd decided to create the spell in a way that it would not be visible for anyone other than those who had the ability to detect magic. This was a secluded but often visited spot and we felt it would be inappropriate to mar the space with what many might consider graffiti.

The charcoal stylus I'd been using to write the spell into the walls left no visible marks. Only through my corrupted vision could I see the faint blue green symbols which made up the locking spell. Slowly I wrote and chanted and waved my hands in circles and arcs and lines that wove the magic into the very crystal that formed the gate between our world and the rift.

After nearly an hour, I'd completed the spell. I knew it was strong. The lock was in place and I tested the lens to verify it worked as predicted. I looked through the lens and saw the five gates. I saw the dozens connected to them. I saw the worlds through which each were interwoven. I could see the darkness of Da Ra Cha Ti at the end of the universe. He had become aware of the absence of Grieta. Soon he would try to become the rift. I could not allow it. I could see him preparing to enter the rift. He used unfocused power to tear open the gate in his place. Soon he would be able to enter. I must get there first if I would have a chance against him.

Quickly, I began to prepare my mind for transition into the rift. Using the lens, I chanted the words that allowed contact.

"Let me see through you. This metal is the same as your metal and they are in harmony. I can see through the mirror I create."

The normal access via the lens seemed to leave my mind blank. I could feel the emptiness in a very palpable way now. I was in contact with the rift but there was nothing there. No feeling of joy, no sense of elation. No peace.

I opened my mind to stretch forth into that empty place. I took a step forward and was gone from the world of men. Once in that dark place, I could see through each of the gates. Those five which were also reflected in thousands of worlds. I began to understand the intertwining of the secondary and tertiary contact points. I could see, if that's the right word, through each and observe a million worlds. I felt desperately alone.

I was reminded of the tales about Tir'na'noth. I decided to focus on the hills behind the causeway. The rift reflected the reality I'd imagined. Though green and beautiful I was alone still. I could look through the gates and sense the tides of people that inhabited the many worlds. But here I was alone.

Then I felt the mind enter. I felt the pain of darkness as it tore into the rift with hatred and anger.

Final Confrontation

Hate can be a physical force. The energy of emotion is the most powerful fuel. In scientific terms there is no loss when converting the darker emotions. Even the residual particles from this action are useful as corruption. They can be used to seed new hate and evil wherever needed. Corruption can be stored and transmitted like a contagion through the hearts and minds of those that seek power at the expense of humanity.

One might have been said to have been corrupt if they took a bribe or broke the rules of government. The true meaning though is more encompassing. Corruption is the metaphysical manifestation of a choice. The desire to go against the betterment of society for the benefit of the self.

There are those that say this is the difference between social ideas and individual freedom. That would not be accurate either. You can enjoy both social peace and personal empowerment without harming others. Corruption is what occurs whenever one person reaches for something while stepping on the neck of another.

What I hadn't really understood till that moment was that it is more real than we'd like to think. You see, death and life are natural. It is even natural for some to live on the death of others. An animal provides nourishment for another animal. The soil is fertilized by the decaying remains of life. There is no corruption in this.

If an act of hatred, emboldened with the emotional power of evil, is perpetrated, corruption is the natural residual of the event.

I felt his anger and the wave of corruption flow through the fabric of the rift.

I expanded my mind to try to encompass the entire rift hoping that I could force the evil from this new body I possessed.

Yes, me possessing a body. An act of possession. I had taken control of this formlessness that I'd once known as Grieta. My mind extended to every corner of creation, feeling the moments as centuries and the centuries as a blink of the eye.

Lights flashed as I could feel the gates interconnected and accessible. I felt the power of a thousand worlds at my beck and call. I felt the stars and the planets charge my purpose. I lost myself for a time.

The light of pain which I could not feel brought me back to the moment. The anger that had started as a tickle in my mind had reformed as hatred and was growing into a burning sensation in a place that was near to what I felt must be my heart.

I reached inward to that place I felt the beating of a gravity. The darkness of a singularity. It drew power from me and corrupted me. I saw the edges speckled with the residual traces of an act of emotional corruption. They spiraled away from the inky center like the arms of a hurricane. I felt the full force of the winds of corruption as they extended into the corners of my mind. Into the corners of the rift.

I would not allow the thing to frame the fight. I must react by altering the dialogue. In that second there stood a tall dark being across the room from me. The room was a cube of equal distance on every side. Light seemed provided from the very air. The dull grey walls of the room sported no doors or windows. There was not even a work of art on any wall.

The dark shape of a man stood some ten feet from me. I could see the glittery blue and red of its eyes as hatred burned from them. The boney clawed hands seemed overlarge. A haze of black smoke seemed to rise upward from the thing in thin tendrils which ended in small spirals of corruption. No details were evident other than the darkness of the shape against the greyness of the room.

It struck with a simple flick of the left wrist. A dagger of black smoke flew toward me from his outstretched hand. I dodged to one side and brought up a barrier spell using only the energy I could access from a nearby nebula. The dagger skidded off my spell, leaving a tear in the spell's protection.

The shape moved again. This time several of the knife blades came in succession. I let the barrier defend me while counterattacking with a ball of light at the center of the darkness. The blades glanced off my defense, leaving it weaker with each contact. My attack spell seemed to have no effect.

I drew upon more resources as I readied another defensive spell. I wanted to build something so strong that it could not be breached. I searched my mind for a way to do this and found nothing except what I'd done already except with more power.

These spells that rely on power can be finessed. I wondered if my enemy would have the imagination necessary to circumvent even a simple barrier spell.

I also realized I must use something a little more imaginative than a ball of light to attack the darkness. Though I was prepared to offer it some of the residual, I decided I would have to resort to something that caused pain.

I constructed it and powered it with the magical energy of a planet not unlike the second world. There was a great deal of energy flowing on that place. It was a virgin world where life had only begun. The power of creation was still new and ever present. I sent the pain at the face of the darkness and was rewarded with an explosion of corruption and the shriek of the thing as it fell away and writhed on the floor of the grey room.

For a moment I gloated over it. I sneered as I saw it jerk and roll in apparent agony. Then I realized that each second I did, a large pool of what can only be referred to as living corruption spread from the thing. Corruption began to radiate from it and through it. In another moment it staggered to its feet, drunk with the power I'd provided.

It didn't shape the energy in any way. The clawed hands reached forth to me and a steady stream of corruption blasted me from each hand. The waves of corruption hit me full in the chest. I felt the power flow into me and begin to subvert me. Slowly, corruption started to replicate the cells of my form and the thought of the mind. If I did nothing to stop it, soon I would be nothing more than a corrupted mentality drifting in the vastness of the rift. And the rift would be Da Ra Cha Ti.

I swept my hands up and used one of the spells of disconnection. These are designed to remove corruption from a host body. In the case of the rift, it blasted the entire place free of corruption for a moment.

The fight was generating corruption though. The longer we battled the more I'd have to clear away even if I won. Corruption was insipient and pervasive. It can hide in places that seem innocent. It can subtly control even the most elemental particle.

I fought for millennium and only for a second. The battle raged as I cast spell after spell drawing upon the most distant galaxies and farthest dimensions for the power and will to destroy the enemy.

My form, which was nothing but an apparition of my own imagination, changed a thousand times. I was a dragon or a lion or a mouse as my will needed me to be. But still neither he nor I could gain the advantage.

He tore at me with claws of black steel and bit into my flesh with fangs red with the blood of millions of souls. Each wound was more fierce and each injury was more lethal. Still I fought on.

He became what I imagined. In one motion a dark pestilence, another a swarm of insects biting and stinging. I knew inside that it was I that shaped the evil and yet still I found deadlier and more threatening forms for it.

How could I win? It was I that powered its aggression. It was my mind that gave it reality. I shaped the evil. I knew then that no matter how I battled, I could not win. The best I might hope for was an eternal conflict at the center of the universe. There it and I would engage in the continuing struggle of good over evil.

The spark of reason came into my mind. I began to understand the truth of the fight. In fighting at all I strengthened it. I gave it all the corruption it needed to continue. It was my own imagination and power of creation that formed its existence in the rift. The rift would offer sources of power that might never be exhausted. All of the power in all of creation was mine to battle it with and to enable it to battle back.

I sought for a way to cut off the flow of energy, to myself and to it. It would make no difference, for in either case Da Ra Cha Ti could not shape the energy I fed him. He could only blast back and bite back with the shapes and forms I'd given him. My mind was the trap. No matter how I tried, I could not unimagine that which I knew was real. In this place I must give it form. The form was a reflection of my fears and hopes. As long as I feared the enemy, I would give it a shape that could harm me.

I tried to give it some innocuous and innocent shape. The small creature I would have imagined seemed a cruel and twisted version as it clawed my face and hands. Somewhere in the dark corners of my mind I could not un-know what a terror the creature was.

I looked around as though I might find some way out of the trap of my own imagination. It seemed ridiculous because I knew that everything here in the rift was as I made it to be. I saw the gates in the distance. Thousands of them and only one. I sifted through them till I found that which I wanted.

I focused on that one gate in the crystal caves under the pointed hill of green. Near the shore, on hexagonal pillars of grey stone stood a small pool of water. By this was the entrance to the rift location.

My friends were there. I looked into the eyes of those I loved and knew that I could never be part of their life as I'd been before. A sadness filled me. I told them of the gates and the world and my thoughts. I said that I loved them all. They could not hear me. I knew that I saw them in my imagination. But was it a sadness that filled them as it did me that last moment before I found the dagger?

In my hand the jeweled Dagger of Thane rested. Its five gems shining just as they had the first time I saw it. In the dream I was a dragon. The mist closed around me and I saw the gold twisted wire of the hilt shine brightly before I gripped it close to my chest.

Maybe this was the only way. The dream I'd had before I began my journey here to the end of my own rainbow. There was no pot of gold. There was no cheering crowd.

I thought back to my youth and remembered the comic books. The hero hid his identity to protect those he loved. Still he fought for them knowing that no one would ever know his sacrifice. I might never see the faces of those I loved again. Perhaps I'd forgotten already. I'd been fighting evil in this place for so long and yet I knew that I'd only just come into the rift.

In a second, those thousands of years had passed. In those thousand years only one heartbeat had pulsed.

My heartbeat. It pulsed in time with the gems on the dagger. Each beat caused a wave of light to run through the weapon while it charged itself for the task at hand.

I moved my mind to the center of the void. I had been here before but it looked unlike the slow flowing river that formed the center of Grieta's consciousness. Instead, it seemed to be a pale ball of light in a vast eddy of swirling colors. I settled there and gripped the thing close again. As the next attack came, I felt the force of my will give the power to do what I must.

I was the rift. I am the center of all things. I will not allow evil to use the rift for its purpose again. I cannot destroy the evil, for in doing so I empower it with corruption. It is without a physical form and therefore it is without the ability to die.

What if...

Yes, that would do...

I was the rift. In a way I had the mind of the void. The void was my thoughts. A possession of a sort. I could allow Da Ra Cha Ti to do the same. We would be joined together as equal parts. Then, if I struck before it realized what I was doing I could end the long struggle. I could finally make sure my world was safe from Da Ra Cha Ti.

I let the darkness in. I opened my mind and invited it to come to the center. Somewhere I reserved just a small place. That was where I hid the dagger.

I felt the darkness flow through me. A glitter of smoky silver blue and red flooded my senses. The mind was terrible and powerful. It came in laughing. It taunted me. It took its pleasure knowing that it had won. It was wrong. Somehow it knew of my plan and tried to take the dagger. In my dream I slipped the dagger between my ribs and deep into my own heart. My heart which was the center. My beating heart which had become the rift. As the rift died, I died, it died.

Darkness.

Promise of the Future

My name is Nick Wills. I have decided to finish this last journal of Chris Jenisen.

I stood in the field where only a few trees gave shade. The tall wiry grass had nearly obscured the small plaque that marked the last resting place of the one that had saved us. As I knelt down to pluck a few blades away from the white stone, I thought of all that had happened.

It has been a few years since we watched him fall to the floor of the crystal cave in Ireland. Though we'd discussed a dozen times, we could not agree on what we thought happened.

Normally a person transitioning through the rift flashes out of our world in a sort of rainbow or aurora of light. Once Chris completed the spell, he stepped forward and simply crumpled to the floor of the cave. We assumed his mind transitioned into the rift. His body was dead.

Only Lucy, who is Grieta, seemed to know but she refused to elaborate more than to tell us that the rift is gone. She explained that Chris must have found that he could not defeat Da Ra Cha Ti. Though she'd hoped he would be able to survive, he'd probably been forced to destroy the rift in order to keep the master of corruption from using it to access our world again.

The gates are all closed and has never been able to be opened again. Though many have tried to access them, there has been nothing but silent waiting at each of the gates.

We've travelled to Asia where the lions still prowl and the temple still stands. The gate there in the dark tunnels beneath remains motionless. In New Mexico we found nothing but a blank wall of stone with a white streak of crystal like strata behind the waterfall. The basement in new England is hiding nothing more than a crack leading to darkness. The geodes are quiet and the crystal cave contains nothing more than large white and purple quartz. There is no rift.

Our job however, has not ended, simply changed. Though Da Ra Cha Ti is no more a threat, his minions still exist. What we once thought might be just a few have turned out to be quite a number. Already we have tracked down several and stopped their evil plans.

Once corrupted, a soul cannot easily be turned back to do good in the world. Darkness is a disease. Corruption may have been used by the enemy but it did not create it. That is our curse. With every dark deed we generate more of the evil stuff.

There were creatures of every sort already in our world when the end of the rift came. Now, though cut off from their master, they seek to reestablish the rule of evil. The vacuum of power has offered the darkest of these beings an opportunity to seek power over the people of our world.

Other creatures simply feed off the death and darkness left in the wake of the Master. Vampire and wraths, wights and spirits still haunt the lonely places of the world. There are still corrupted dead in the world. It has become our mission to battle them as well.

New creatures have been created. There are a few that understand the ways of darkness and corruption and use it to build their own evil plans.

There are even creatures from other worlds still hiding in the darkness waiting for who knows what. When we find them, we destroy them.

The funeral for Chris Jenisen was attended by only the few of us that knew him best.

Arianna spoke about her love for him and her wish that they could have shared a life together. Min spoke of his strength of character which gave her hope for tomorrow. Hector told us about his unwavering friendship which he showed by the constant sacrifices he'd made for us. Maria spoke of his compassion even though he didn't know how to show it, she'd seen him cry at the deaths of her family. Conner spoke of his intellect, of which he was so proud.

I didn't say anything though I thought of the soft sweet music that had once played on a dark night in the jungles of Asia. I remembered his head had been bowed and I thought I saw a smile on his face as one tear fell. He'd led us and taught us. He'd been the glue that held us together.

Though he is gone, the memory of his last actions still keep the team going. Conner and Maria are our leaders. They send us out into the world to battle what evil still exists. Hector, Min, Lucy, Arianna and I are the soldiers in the fight.

There are others who fight, to be sure, but we are the ones that take the brunt of the battle. We've lost a few and won a few. Our ranks are growing. A new generation is learning to wage the war. Min and Hector have two children now. Though young, they are beginning to understand their role in the world.

Maria and Conner are also parents of two very amazing young children. Their second was a daughter which they have named Chris after the one that saved us all.

My name is Nick Wills. I was a soldier before and I'm a soldier again. Though the enemy changes, the battle goes on.

Gunslinger

The being was standing in what seemed to be an open area now only twenty yards ahead. Its legs spread wide, and its arms hung in the shape of long hooks to its sides. It seemed slightly hunched.

"There you are," It laughed. "I have you finally. This time on my own terms." The harsh scratchy voice forced open the memory of Seattle.

Nick responded by shooting twice into its chest.

The thing looked down at the holes as glittery dust fell gently from the injury. It then looked at Nick with a smile and drew and fired its old style revolver.

Corrupted croc

As it cleared the door frame its shape came into focus. the long winding body on four short stilts of legs, was obviously a crocodile. There was some disturbing deformity of the spine and head that included several rows of broken spike like projections that seemed both familiar and terrifying. In the gloom a green and silver glitter could be seen shining in the small eyes. Elongated and curved claws now jutted several inches from the humanlike hands and feet. At the end of the tail several of the ridges jutted upward like the spikes on a stegosaurus.

Wight

The man seemed Asian though his skin was somewhat pale. His hair seemed bleached and almost pure white. If it were not for the smooth youthful complexion he might have been mistaken for an old man. The dark circles around his eyes and hollowed cheeks lent a sinister aspect.

There are literally dozens of undead creatures in the world. Vampires, ghosts, wraiths, and may more have been created by the forces of evil. Some are tools of the Master, others are simply creatures of evil fighting to survive and feed in a world of the living. There are a few that believe they can regain their humanity by devouring the life force or even the flesh of those that are without corruption. Such is a wight.

The mentality of the creature is bonded to a recently deceased body. If it feeds on the flesh of the living quickly, it can stop the body from rotting away.

legend says that if it consumes enough uncorrupted flesh, the wight can regain its humanity.

Corrupted corps

The enemy was composed of several dozen creatures in a variety of states of decomposition. Most seemed freshly minted and had very little to indicate they'd become servants of corruption other than the blank look of the recently dead. Others seemed several weeks into their quietus and had obviously limited time left to serve the master.

Devourer

Large heavy arms reached through the demolished panel and grabbed him. At the touch he seemed to whither. His body stiffened and the luster in his eyes was replaced with a blue white gloss. His facial skin shrank and dried as his lips stretched back revealing teeth yellowed from age. He fell to the floor landing with a heavy thump. A Devourer!

When a devourer comes into a new world it shape-changes till it finds a form that offers the most potential in whatever environment it encounters. This one seemed to be a cross between a gorilla and a spider. Its face sported the general appearance of a gorilla with a dozen lidless spot eyes.

It stood nearly ten feet in height. The long forearms seemed heavy at the apex of the elbow. The fists were the size of a football helmet. Eight appendages resolved to four arms and four legs. The barrel shaped human torso sported a large round belly and a heavy four lobed chest. The back jutting abdomen was supported on four legs flipped up and angled in the shape of a spider. Though large and round, each section seemed well muscled and thickly boned.

The Master (Da Ra Cha Ti)

The dark shape of a man stood some ten feet from me. I could see the glittery blue and red of its eyes as hatred burned from them. The boney clawed hands seemed overlarge. A haze of black smoke seemed to rise upward from the thing in thin tendrils which ended in small spirals of corruption. No details were evident other than the darkness of the shape against the greyness of the room.

Made in the USA
San Bernardino, CA
04 March 2017